Oct 2, 2021

THE
FAREWELL
TOUR

Dear Jackie & Carla —
My girls!! Thanks for
stopping by & thanks for reading

Karen Bennett

THE FAREWELL TOUR

a novel

Karen S. Bennett

In Appreciation

*My thanks goes out for the "go gettum" support from the many
in Baltimore's community of writers.*

And, especial thanks to Tom Selburg, my computer repairman.

Much appreciation to Paige Akins for her

interal design, expert and willing help.

Contents

CHAPTER 1

MY LAST DAY

February 1998

The sagging, foreign bed creaked as I pressed one hand to my low back, winced, and rolled into the strip of sunlight. I rocked forward with an, "Ooof," and swung my feet to the floor. "Today's the day, February the fifth, in the year of our Lord, 1998, and we're off!"

Two noisy birds in a domestic quarrel knocked dry plant fronds against the hotel's window frame, only inches from my sill. I opened the unpainted shutters and squinting into the early morning answered the birds' chattering discontent. "You two had better cut that out. Do you know what today is? Huh, do you?" The chastised birds retreated into India's morning sky, leaving behind a swirl of small black feathers.

"This is IT! At last. I don't know whether to be happy or sad. If the fates are doing what I think they are doing," I sighed and gave the depressed pillow a fluffing pat and announced to the empty room, " ... I'll never have to make up a bed again. Ever.

"Ughhh, it's so hot already. And bright." I blew a stream of cool breath between my damp nightgown and my skin. The air is almost too hot to draw in a deep breath. "How do the people of this country stand this constant heat?" I wiped perspiration from my forehead, pulled the sheets to the top of the bed, and slapped wrinkles from the thin bedspread. Satisfied, I stood back and laughed, noticing the side table holding a pitcher, full of water, without the detail of a drinking glass. I consulted the iridescent numerals on my watch, that showed it was time to be on to my next, and last adventure.

My hair, sparked with gray, was cut coquettishly short, per the advertisement on the hairdresser's wall back in Pennsylvania; "Perfect for summer travel, maximize your vacation, carefree beauty." My morning toilet was complete with a few swipes of my hair, and *voila, fait accompli.*

On this special day I dressed in khaki, knee length shorts. No silk or satiny gown of fine beauty for today. Rocking up on the toes of my hiking boots, I looked backwards at my buttocks, appraised the spidery veins of my 56-year-old legs, shrugged, and yanked at my baggy shorts, celebrating that on this special day, I could be anywhere and I was in India, and I could be wearing anything, and I was in khaki. Hallelujah!

The colorful embroidered flowers on the light blue shirt were all the adornment I'd need today. Blue socks topped my leather boots. Jewelry, unnecessary. I stepped back to appraise myself in a narrow mirror, with most of the silver gone from its back. Ah, the perfect ballooning adventure outfit.

I clapped my hand on the left back pocket to confirm the presence of folding money and credit card, then poked my arm through the loops of the purple nylon shoulder bag and the canvas backpack. My stubborn passport refused to fit into the same pants pocket. Annoyed, I sat on the bottom end of the bed, opened the small document and examined the thing. I look nice enough. I guess this is the photo they'll publish on the obituary page in Pine Bluffs. At least it's an improvement over my last passport picture with the lesion of an American eagle embossed across my face. I asked the photo, "When was the last time I was pleased with a picture of myself? Never." After a few moments of studying my face, I exhaled an acceptance, flapped the passport shut, slipped the packet into the square, plastic envelope and into the buckled pocket on the leg of my khakis it went. I stood to go.

Turning to have a last look at the worn, tasseled throw rug next to the narrow bed, I thought how one could say this was where a lunatic artist or a famous philanthropist, or celebrated poet spent her last night. The room was as forlorn and historic as those rooms I'd seen roped off when I and the Girl Scouts went to historic, dead peoples' houses.

In the hotel lobby, I greeted the solitary hotel clerk, who was trussed up to his buttoned neck in a wilted, white shirt, closed with a black bow tie. He bowed, then confirmed in perfect English, the departure time of the bus from this location to the balloon ride pick- up at the Rose River depot. I wish I spoke two languages as easily as the clerk did. Oh well, too late.

I dumped my luggage to the floor in front of a carved teak table and took a Styrofoam cup of warm syrupy tea from a well-polished samovar decorated with curlicues. I laughed at not seeing a samovar when I visited Russia, but here at this dusty crossroads in India stood a glossy beauty.

I gingerly touched the hot vessel, admiring its elegance. Hotels at home should hide their utilitarian, ugly coffee, and hot water urns.

I reminisced, wondering if this emotion was a twinge of home sickness. I was so very far from Pine Bluffs, and missed my breakfast table. "Buck-up, girl," I mumbled. "You've gone to a lot of trouble and expense *to not* be at home. So, enjoy this experience."

Remembering I no longer had to worry about calorie counting, I scooped up a dry biscuit from a pyramid of baked goods. I'd tasted two biscuits yesterday and knew them to be flaky and sweet, flavored with almond and a hint of cinnamon, a good breakfast choice. Today I carried the biscuit in an open paper napkin, careful to not lose a crumb as I picked up my luggage, and stepped outside to the unpaved street.

I heard music. "Could that be, '*The Mighty Quinn*?' Yes, that was it." Two teen-aged boys sat in an open Land Rover, pounding their knuckles on the dashboard, and bouncing their heads, accompanying the tune. "I'll bet the song is about cocaine. I'm sure India is no stranger to cocaine."

With some fear about the unknown adventures ahead, I was buoyed up by the daily unexpected entertainment and satisfaction from this great vacation. I bit into my biscuit while settling on a sunny bench next to two stripped down bicycles propped against a deteriorating concrete and stone wall. A half-naked old man, as bony as the pedicab he pedaled, zipped past. His eyebrows went up and his mouth opened in an apologetic 'O' when his speed caused a spray of pebbles to pelt my legs. He kept riding.

"Yow!" I hopped up and checked my legs for blood. None. I rubbed my stung skin, and retreated to the sparse shade of a spreading tree where I comforted the injured little girl within me with a satisfying foreign breakfast. I peeled and ate an orange, then finished off two dusty cashews hiding in the bottom of a backpack pocket. Still smarting from the indignity of the stinging pebbles, I opened my shoulder bag and produced a four-inch, waxed paper wrapped square of sticky, pounded apricot, a treat with an Indian name I could not pronounce. After licking the biscuit's powdered sugar from my fingers, I reached into another of the many zipper pockets of my backpack and withdrew a small, lined tablet. I produced a ball point pen, clicked the tip, then leaning the tablet on my lap, I started my newest entry, *My Very Last Day*. 2-5-98.

CHAPTER 2

PINE BLUFFS

November 1997

Pine Bluffs, Pennsylvania's census was increased in 1942 with my birth, and again in 1944 when my little sister, Lily was born. We obedient little girls were given a warm and safe home, tap dance lessons, and were sent to Sunday School and Girl Scouts. We completed our public school, then college studies, and in the end came back to the Keystone State to marry and raise our own families. I married Jerry Schuler, a well cut, serious fellow who owned an industrial laundry business. We had one daughter, Kimmy, a great girl. She went on to marry and repeat the process. Her daughter, Sara, is my only grandchild, another great little girl who looks like her mom, but is blonder. My sister, Lily's and my own family all settled on our parents' street, with the younger generation enjoying ballet, scouts, baseball and softball. Lily and Stan's two sons and their two grandsons are all now living in other states where their jobs have taken them.

Before being sent into the world of elementary school, Lily and I were obliged to memorize our phone number and address. Our family's phone number was 2598, plain and simple; four-digits. Jumping forward forty years, all adults found themselves in need of a four-digit secret access number, a numeric password, the PIN, the Personal Identification Number, to access the machines containing various accounts. I chose our family's old phone number, 2598, confident no thief or swindler would connect my important PINs with a phone number from my childhood.

Over the years, I began to notice the same four numbers sort of following me around. Not sensible, but no denying it either. My college ID number was 2598-60. The 60 was for the year of my college entrance, and I guessed the 2598 was the work of the gods. My marriage certificate number ended with those four-digits in sequence, as did my present gas/electric account number. After my husband died, my brazen new bank account began with 2598. In the long run, the appearance of the sequential digits became expected, and did not disappoint.

*

Here begins my story. In early November 1997, on what started as a typical day, my life shot-off from my familiar orbit. I'd pulled my car up to the garage door's PIN pad and tapped in 2, 5, 9, and 8. The door obediently rolled up. I put the car to bed and closed the door.

Back in the house, the phone's answering machine was blinking, indicating a waiting message. Bouncing my finger to the 2, 5, 9, and 8 on the keypad, I heard my daughter, Kimmy's recorded voice. "Mom, Sara has something important to tell you." The phone had been handed over to my little pride and joy. Sara's gleeful childish voice celebrated, "Grandmom, you won the candy! Your number was the winner. Guess what Grandmom, you get to keep all the M&Ms. Can we have some too, Grandmom? Huh? Can we? Mommy says I have to hang up now. Good-bye, I love you. Don't forget, we get to keep the candy."

"Well, would you look at that! Old 2598 came through again. Too bad I didn't spend the money on a lottery ticket. Guess I'll be giving away gift-wrapped packets of M&Ms for Christmas this year."

Back in November, with my granddaughter jumping next to me, I wrote the number 2598 on a piece of paper as my best guess at the number of M&Ms in a very large jar, and paid a dollar for the Pioneer Girls' fundraiser. Celebration time! No wonder Sara was excited. I laughed and agreed with myself that something in the neighborhood of 2,598 is a hell of a lot of M&Ms. I wonder if that was the exact number of the candies, or the closest guess to 2,500 or 3,000.

I shared the good news on the phone with my sister. "Hey Lily, I'm rich! It wasn't the Three State Lottery, but I've gone up in Sara's estimation since I won almost three thousand M&Ms." We laughed at the child's good luck.

I continued in my musing to my little sister. "The dirty truth is I also submitted a guess for 4,000 candies, along with another dollar, but that guess was wrong. It makes you think."

"About what?"

"About the number 2598?"

"What about it?" I could visualize Lily blinking her eyes.

"Haven't I mentioned the uptick in appearances of 2598, our old phone number? You know, I use those digits for all my PINs. I swear, Lily, the numbers are following me around. I had to laugh last week when Kimmy's and my lunch check was a nice, neat, $25.98. Need I remind you, that's the winning number for the candy too? It's almost creepy except the numbers so far have been benign, but screamingly coincidental. I wonder if they're foretelling something. What's left in my life for those numbers to predict? What's the emergency?"

Lily said, "Well, 2598 was the whole family's phone number. Except now there's the addition of the area code and the exchange. I can't imagine the numbers got together in a meeting and decided to follow you around, Beverly."

"Ah-haaah! That's it!" My index finger shot up into the air, an orator's posture. Here came the truth; "Of course! But, nah, it's too ridiculous."

"What? What's 'it'? What's too ridiculous?" she asked.

"Huh? Lily, you still there?" I looked around, distracted, already moving on in my head.

"Of course I'm still here. We haven't exactly hung up yet."

"Hang up, Lily, I've gotta go." I crashed the phone to its cradle. Fizz, my cat shot from my lap as if the starter's bullet fired and someone yelled, "And they're off!" Both hands came up to my face, pushing my surprise back into my mouth. I jumped up and sucked in a deep breath. "Holy cow!"

A faraway look came over me. I was torn between the appreciation at the consistency of the numbers and at the same time was somewhat surprised at what I was sure they portended. "No, it's a huge, big, fat coincidence. That's all."

I argued with myself, always a fruitful activity. "Not a coincidence, a sign. At last, the numbers make perfect sense." The cool parent in my head was tamping down my new hysteria saying, "coincidence, happenstance, a queer, little funny thing. Damn!"

I was on my feet, pacing a tight circle in the living room trying to reason with myself. "Beverly, you're nuts to be thinking like this. Yes, I am. I should be scared. It's preposterous. No, it's obvious." I stood, feet spread, both hands palms upward at my sides, indicating the obvious for the world to see. The refrigerator's noisy motor clicked on to join my celebration of my insight and talking. "Maybe the numbers were like a guardian angel, to keep me mindful of their constant presence. Oh, that's ridiculous, but look, they're still showing up everywhere." Imploring the cat's cooperation and agreement, I said, "But, is it coincidence, Fizzy? Could it be?" Fizzy gave no answer, and seeing no food in his dish, flagged his tail straight up and left the room.

I turned back to the jury in my head. "Lily will think I've gone ABsoLUTEly bonkers. I can't tell Kimmy. She'd have me institutionalized. She already suspects my senility." No, it'll be a secret, though I'll need to tell Lily. I mean, she's my sister, she'll deserve some explanation, and I'll need a conspirator, somebody in cahoots with me. The refrigerator, apparently satisfied with my epiphany shut off with a muffled rumble.

I went to bed, but couldn't sleep. I flipped from front to back and punched my pillow. My mind was going at full tilt. I guess this is what insanity must feel like. I grabbed my hair,

11

and shaking my head, testing for craziness, said, "Maybe *I AM* crazy." I blurted, "Oh, I can read it now. 'Local woman goes stark, raving mad after winning over 2,500 M&Ms in a Pioneer Girl fund-raiser.'" Again Fizz's reverie was interrupted. He was jettisoned to his feet from a peaceful sleep as I threw back the blankets and made the sudden change from repose to standing next to the bed. "Sorry, cat." Then I addressed the roses on the wallpaper, "This makes perfect sense. Heck, you can't argue with the numbers. It's so obvious." My mind was racing. "Two-five-nine-eight is an upcoming date!" An answer flew into my mind. Hey, that's February the 5th, 1998, and it's only three months away, and the numbers are leading me. Dragging me."

I shot a look at the digital, bedside clock, saw the glowing two and twelve and sighed, "Forget sleeping. Time is shooting by." I flicked on the light, wrapped myself in my plaid bathrobe, and tapped my basset hound slipper on the carpet. I straightened and raised an index finger to explain my philosophy, "I'm pleased, and relieved to be in control of my life. Now, I'll plan my life, that will not include a sad, little dying episode in Pine Bluffs."

I held the closet door open with my bulky dog slipper and pulled the flattened aubergine suitcases still in their plastic wrap from the high shelf. They were to be a birthday gift to Kimmy in April. "Ahhh, Kimmy, dear daughter, I'll have to leave you something else. These suitcases are mine now." The advertisement on the plastic wrap boasted, feather light and resilient. "Yup, that's precisely what I'll need, 'feather light'. I looked at the overhead light and hollered, "Yahoo," like a wolf celebrating the moon. Once again

I was glad to live alone where no dissatisfied person rolled his eyes at me. "What will Lilly think? I'm out of my mind? Maybe I am, but it's so logical. Why didn't I recognize these numbers as a date years ago?"

I stretched rapid strides down the hall, down the stairs, and to the kitchen. I pulled a tablet from the messy kitchen drawer. An advertisement for 'Palmer's Hardware and More' ran across the top of the tablet. Jerry's old mug, with some lame angler pun painted on its side, was filled with pens, pencils and old scissors. "Okay, here's the plan." I snapped up a ballpoint pen, moving about the kitchen in a flurry of excitement. I turned the radio on, then off, then on, then off again.

"I can't ignore the signs, Fizzy," directed to my cat's back. He curled on papers piled on a kitchen chair, and rebuffed my attention.

I poured some tea, and slipped the stack of mail from under the curled cat. "I have to give you credit, Fizzy. You can sleep through anything." I fingered the envelope I knew to contain information on my widow's benefits. This is real. I'm a widow. I'm alone. Now get on with it.

I tore open the envelope in a way that always made Jerry angry. My theory was, who cares, the envelope goes right into the trash, right? Wrong answer. Jerry's law was the envelope was to be preserved to document the date the item was mailed. How long will his chastisement of me and my imperfect ways plague me from his ashes at the mausoleum? I pitched the envelope to the trash. Hah! I missed.

Next, I opened the final bill for the home loan for the new patio and noted, with a laugh that the total was

$25.98. "Well, would you look at that. I don't know whether to laugh or cry." I was silent, shook my head, and stared straight ahead. "These numbers mean business." Squinting his eyes shut, Fizz smiled at me. He purred and swished his tail, knocking a few envelopes to the floor. "Thanks a lot. You're the kind of help I need around here."

I jumped up and pulled my shapeless blue sweater from the back of my chair. I wrapped the flat arms around me for the hug I needed. "Everything that happens in a lifetime; grow up, get a job, get married, have a kid, have a grandchild, retire, be widowed, has already happened. What's left?"

I knew. I sucked in a deep breath. Yes, that's all it could mean. I grabbed the chair. The room spun. My words reverberated. I leaned to the table as my brain cautioned, "Don't faint, don't faint."

I flopped down into the chair and laughed. Uninvited tears trickled down. I startled myself with a loud gasp. Words came bubbling up from my subconscious. "That's it. Two-five-nine-eight is the date I'm going to die! My death date is coming up in 90 days."

I stared for a while then heard from the angel on the left shoulder. "I'm healthy and young. Why would I die?

The right shoulder angel answered, "Oh! Maybe an accident."

My eyebrows shot up at this unwelcome insight. I wonder if it'll hurt. Will I linger? I've got a lot to think about." Gravity replaced my heady joy. I swiped at tears. I'd better go back to bed." I rose from the table, turned out the lights and scuffed up stairs. Fizzy followed.

CHAPTER 3

DEBATE THE DATE

Morning sunlight, too new to be robust, fell across my face. I rubbed my head and said, "What's next?" The clock radio provided orchestral background to the reprise of last night's thoughts.

"What happened yesterday?" I was smacked by a realization, against all sense and all odds, that a force was moving me toward the date of 2-5-98. "Why? What do I want? Happiness for my family. I've had a good life. An easy life."

I rolled to my side and pondered, speaking my thoughts, slowly, deliberately. "If I had to write my own 'Rules for Death,' I'd specify I don't want to die here, in ho-hum, little, vanilla, Pine Bluffs' unremarkable hospice, with IVs and a bunch of tubes and bags attached to me. I don't want my sad, silent family gathered around wondering whose job it will be to sell the furniture and the house, and who will take the cat?

"I don't want my anemic obituary to say I died far too young, at fifty-five of, well, whatever, with nothing interesting to say." I sat up. "Where have I traveled? Nowhere. What was my fascinating job? Teacher to Pine Bluffs' fifth graders. I mean, I liked the kids, but, kill me now." My head dropped back into my pillow. I pulled the blankets over my face and groaned, "I understand why Nobel made a conscious decision to change his life from refining nitro-glycerine to the celebration of Peace.

"Maybe the date means, ahhh, maybe, ahhh,.." my respirations deepened. I swung my arm over my eyes to darken the room and slid back to sleep. Fizzy played along and joined in for a spontaneous nap. Later, missing his breakfast, he mobilized me by drilling his feet into my chest, a never fail technique.

If this were happening to anyone else, my advice would be to make the best of it. Do things. Go places. Clean out. Close up. Sell, donate, move on, prepare." I pounded my right fist into my left palm. "Hey! That sounds good. I should plan a trip. Do everything, go everywhere I can afford. End all diets. Eat cake."

Presently I was on my feet. Bathroom, quick shower, into clothes, down to the kitchen for breakfast; tea and a piece of peach pie. I grabbed a pencil and made a list, spouting ideas faster than I could write. I hopped up at intervals to run into the cellar, to the garage, to the attic, mumbling as I went, keeping a mental inventory.

"Donate the ping pong table to the Salvation Army. Give the stack of calico squares for quilting to the Pioneer Girls. Have a garage sale in January, oh, and at last, get rid of that gawdawful, darned trampoline out back. Give it to a friend or, better yet, to an enemy. Oh, this is great. Those jars of strawberry and rhubarb can go to the church for their many dinners. Christmas is a-coming and I can off-load some heirlooms."

I sat hard on the back porch top step, pulling the jacket's collar to my ears. "If I smoked, this is where I'd take a

16

significant, deep drag on my cigarette." I stared at the white sky. "Jerry died in 1995. I guess I've fulfilled the polite, public period for mourning." I clapped my hands in one loud punctuation and stood. "He's been dead long enough for me to clean out the last of his stuff. I know of no one who wants his fishing gear, so, hallelujah, I'll cart his fishing tackle to the donation box. Thank God. And, I can stop being a widow now, and get on with what's left of my own life. No more boo-hooing."

Lily showed up for her usual visit of afternoon dessert and chat. I was distracted, moving about the kitchen, not sitting until she said, "I didn't walk all the way, past three houses to sit here and watch you run around. What's up with you today?"

I slid into my chair like sliding into second base, without the dust. Her eyebrows shot up. In lifelong familiarity, we propped our elbows on the checkered tablecloth, picking up on yesterday's subject.

"Lily, something giant has happened. Don't judge. Let me talk."

She sat straight, folded her hands on the tabletop and made an, "I'm listening" face at my many false starts.

I sighed, looked down at my own hands, then stated, "The skin on my hands is getting thinner, the veins are becoming more prominent, exactly like Mom's." Lily prepared to make her rejoinder, but I shushed her with my index finger to my lips. I claimed the floor, "Which brings me to my topic for today. Lily, what I have to say, well it's crazy-different, that's for sure. Look Lily, I have to die *sometime*."

She stopped chewing the walnut covered sticky bun in mid bite, and gave a polite smile. She tilted her head in a listening posture, as it was clear I was now ready for her input. She emptied her tea cup. She shook the napkin from her lap, smoothed the wrinkles, and refolded the thing.

I blurted, "I think, bear with me, I think '2598' is a date and I think it's my death date." There! I said it. "So, before I die I'm taking a trip, a long one."

"Bev, are you nuts? '2598' doesn't *mean* anything. They're a string of numbers. Period. Their showing up is random, that's all."

I knew that, but, I also knew I was right and shifted my eyes.

Lily reloaded, "I can't believe we're having this conversation. I've always respected you, even worshipped you as the older sister, but, Honey, I'm afraid you've gone around the bend." She took a deep breath to refuel, then returned to the fray. "You're crazy. Not counting this stunning conclusion of yours, don't you think it's odd that you've always talked to yourself? Not a good omen."

I answered. "Are you kidding? I wasn't talking to myself. You overheard me all those times talking to Jerry. He never answered. Did you think I was talking to myself?" I paused, and owned up to the hurt. I was sheepish, but joking came to the rescue, "Once in a while, I do talk to myself. I get such excellent answers."

"Beverly Ruth, you expect me to suspend belief in the real word and agree that the number of candies in a jar dictates your death date? You're cracked. Your daughter uses your same four numbers for her codes too. Kimmy's exact words, when she moved into her first apartment were, 'I use Mom's code so I don't have to think up another one.'"

"You know kids, too lazy to come up with their own darned PIN. But, Lily, the four numbers don't show up for anybody else. Only for me. I'm sure little Sara would agree. The heck with every one of those over two thousand and five hundred M&Ms, they were the latest in a series of those same numbers showing up."

Lily countered, "Then maybe, Bev, if you're looking for coincidence, maybe February the fifth is when Kevin and Kimmy get pregnant again. How about that? Or, I hate to say it, but have you considered you're having a belated grief reaction to Jerry's death? Maybe, simply maybe, this is plain old grief and unconsciously you're going for that desperate grasp at life?" She clamped her lips, having delivered a succinct little insight.

"Grieving over Jerry? I'm grieving, but not because he's gone, but because he was a pill, and a grump, and uncooperative, and unsupportive, and I doubt he even *liked* me. And, I've been mad at him for twenty years. He never showed that side to you. But you'll remember he always cleared out of the room, lickety-split, when you and I were together. I lived with him all those years pretending, even believing things were good. If I've shocked you, it's to demonstrate that suspecting I have a date to die has nothing to do with Jerry."

Feeling the need to lighten the mood, I leaned back and reached behind me for my purse on the shelf. I plunked the bag onto my lap and pulled two singles from the wallet. "I'll tell you what, Lily, here are two dollars. Buy me a lottery

ticket on 2-5-98. Wait… ," waving a tenner in her face, "…
here's a ten dollar bill. It'll be my lucky day, so make it good.
Buy, Buy!"

I warmed up for one more argument. "Last Thursday
a little old lady in line in front of me at the bank told how
she was moving money from one of the interest bearing
accounts to another in order to earn a little money. Lily,
that old girl should be spending her money, travel, do what
she always wanted to do. Heck, our only darned guarantee is we might spend our last days in Pine Bluffs General
Hospital attached to machines. Who wouldn't come off
their, you should pardon the expression, their death bed
to dip into their 401K if they foresaw the bleak death the
fates had in store for them? Don't you think most husbands
would work in some meaningful gesture, or buy a gift for
his wife if he had any clue he was about to die? Don't you
think Jerry might have been kinder to me if he'd known he
would have an out-and-out, one-time fatal stroke at the age
of fifty-eight?

"For Heaven's sake, Lily, look around. People are dying
and most of them left money in the bank for second wife
who wasn't there for the earning of the money. Grown children with their own 401Ks are inheriting the hard won savings of the forebears. I mean, that's nice for them, but what
about the guy who earned it? I worked and saved all my
life and I'll die. Where's my fun and the enjoyment that I
deserve for earning, and *saving* the money to begin with?
What is going to happen to *your* savings, Lily?" I didn't wait
for her answer. With the worst of taste, I continued, "Kids,
grandkids, and Stan going to divvy it up? Stan can buy a

nice new car so he looks good when he goes to Friday night dances down at the Elks Club to look for his new wife." I slapped my hand to my mouth to cover-up my last words, a little nasty, all things considered. "Sorry, Lily, that was ugly. I didn't mean anything. Stan's a great husband to you."

She was defused by my impassioned rebuttal. Her own arguments paled against mine, I must confess. She leaned her elbow on the table, and made little swirly patterns on the checkered tablecloth with the fork tines. She didn't look up at me. "So, you're spending your own money with the intent of seeing the world, turning over new stones, to give the obituary readers a better story?"

I shot back, "Well, yeah. Aw, come on. You know that's not what I meant."

Lily looked up, still toying with the silverware. "The thought is intriguing. Very daring."

I shot back, "You're darned tootin'. Don't you see the 2598 Theory as an interesting and infectious thought?" I tapped a finger on my cheek in a mock 'thinking' manner. "Hmmm. Spend your own money on yourself. Hmmm. Or leave it for someone else?" Both palms turned up as I weighed both options. I paused. It was time to mollify. I bent to look right into her eyes. "You and I are going to have one hell of a good laugh on February the sixth. And, thereafter too."

Her head snapped up. Her fork clanked to the plate.

"You've overlooked something! Two-five-nine-eight can't be a date," she crowed in a superior voice. "Because, to be technical, February the fifth would be written,

'ZERO-two-ZERO-five-nine-eight.'" She flopped back in her chair as if to say, "I have spoken."

"Call it what you will. Suppose this were happening to you." I tapped the ball back to my little sister. "Think about it. I'm closing up and traveling."

Silence all around.

I waited then whispered, "Pregnant pause. Lily, I thought I had this all figured out, but I forgot how you would feel." I leaned to within two inches of my sister's nose, "Honey, do you want to come with me for part of my trip? Would Stan agree to you taking a little vacation with me? How about coming along for a week or two? Come on Lily-O. We'll have fun. Come to Alaska and see the Aurora Borealis with me. You'd like that, wouldn't you?"

"No, Dearheart, somebody with a different PIN has to stay home and feed Fizz and buy the lottery tickets, and gloat at the airport when you come home, broke." She twisted her chair away from the table and walked to the window as if something outside had caught her attention. She scooped up Fizzy who had been pressed up next to the radiator and held him near her face. She whispered a compliment into his ear. I sat and waited.

With tears in her voice she said, "Bev, you're giving me the same empty, helpless, and hollow feeling I had when Daddy died." She stood, dropped the cat on her chair and pressed her fist into the space below her breast bone. I looked away without an argument.

"Last question, Beverly Ruth Schuler." Yikes, she was calling me by my whole name. "Have you changed your will?"

I laughed, "I'm keeping some of the money from the sale of Jerry's business. The remainder will go to Kimmy, of course. She, Kevin, and Sara will have plenty to spend. They'll be envious of my vacation. If I come home, ... ahhh," I reworked the beginning of the sentence to eliminate *if.* "I have to answer this wanderlust before I come home again. You do understand, don't you, Lily-O?"

She sighed, "Great. I've got to go. I need to pick out a new dress for your funeral. We'll talk later, but no more today." Tears wetted her face as she slipped her arms into her ski jacket. I caught up with her at the door. "You're worried and truthfully, I'm scared too. But, I can't stay home, I can't." We air-kissed good-bye and she dashed from the porch, to four doors down the street.

I closed the back door when I saw my sister's foot disappear behind the line of bushes that edged her property. I leaned against the closed door to ponder the sad turn the visit had taken. "She'll be all right. I guess the kindest thing toward Lily is to pretend I'll be coming home again. Who can say? Who can read my future?" I took a deep breath then answered, "The numbers!"

A thick pause dropped to the floor like pudding, then I whooped a joyful tune to the front hall, "Hurray, I'm going to have the best obituary! Whoo-hoo."

CHAPTER 4

FAREWELL FARE

On the following day, with my dining room table cluttered with various tourist brochures, the yellow lined tablet, and the mug of pencils, I got busy. The cat thought the mess of papers was specifically strewn for his sleeping comfort. I'd laid out the catalogues in travel sequence. I paged through one of Kimmy's old high school textbooks searching for maps of Russia. The whole continent-wide country of Russia offers mainly Moscow and Saint Petersburg for tourists. I wished I had more time. Oh well. All would be great. I tapped my pen against my projected itinerary. Russia for close to ten days. There's plenty to see and do there. Once on the other side of the world, all my other visits would be in the same hemisphere, so, India would be local. And, it's my money, so who's counting? Okay, that's settled. I reached for the pencil and scribbled across the itinerary, "after February 5th, maybe see Vietnam."

The pencil tip snapped. My heart jumped. I stopped abruptly, blinked and whispered, "Ohhh! Gads, look at that. I guess I *will* die on the fifth." My hand flew to the flutter in my heart. "Otherwise why else would the pencil point break? Yikes." I wiped at a sudden tear and directed my commentary to the cat, "This is real." I pondered for a moment and concluded, "I guess this is what Lily meant when she accused me of talking to myself. The girl is right."

It was afternoon dessert time when Lily called from the front door and entered balancing a fluffy white coconut cake. "Yikes. Where's your tabletop? What a mess of scattered papers. Where shall I put this cake? Kitchen?"

"Yes, please. Five minutes ago, I received a call from the travel agent. Cheaper to go to Saint Petersburg, Russia and not such a big deal to get a visa. Funny, huh? Why are some places harder to visit than others? Hot Damn! The wheels are in motion now!"

I held up the list of countries in the order of travel, with nothing written after February the fifth. I slipped the return ticket home to Philadelphia for the fourteenth of February next to the itinerary, knowing Lily would see the return ticket. That should shut her up.

Lily held up an envelope of twenty, 3 x 4-inch, net bags in various pastels, with ribbon ties. "Here are the little bags we talked about. What's the emergency for them to go on your trip, pray tell."

I laughed and reached to her hand. "Give them here. Hurry up. I have to hide them before Sara gets here. I'm not so sure she'd approve of the plan where I distribute small gift bags of M&Ms about the world. The candy will increase my luggage weight, but only until I get going. I'll leave them with busboys, maids, et cetera." I grabbed the envelope and hurried them off to my suitcases.

When I returned to the dining room table Lily was paging through the text books. She looked up over her glasses. "What on earth makes you want to go to India? You never mentioned India before." She looked up nonchalantly, fingering the return ticket.

"I never mentioned a lot of things. What would have been the point? Jerry would have, and did say "No," to anything I suggested.

"Anyway, don't you remember those Madras plaids we wore in seventh and eighth grades? They were everywhere. The boys had shirts in the Madras plaid and I had a skirt and vest, dark blue and inky black. You had a shirtwaist dress in a lighter blue. Don't you remember that?"

She blinked. "Nope. And I can't imagine why any out-of-style fabric would send you on a quest around the world."

I looked to the ceiling for patience. "I've always been intrigued, and I want to go. You know, curries, wildly decorated buses, the elephant god. Should be great." I changed the subject. "My first scheduled stop is Alaska. You should come with me. We'd have fun. Alaska could include a dog-sled ride, and with luck we'd see the Aurora Borealis. You'd like that wouldn't you? They say the best chance of seeing the northern lights is in Fairbanks in February. The best I can do is to be in Fairbanks in January. But, since the aurora isn't performed by union workers, perhaps I'll get lucky and see it off schedule."

I smiled my best used car salesman smile. "Of course I've always wanted to go up in a hot air balloon, though I still don't know where that'll be. Best guess is India. I'll wear plaid. Or maybe the balloon will be plaid." I laughed, but Lily didn't.

Lily fired up, "What? No human cannonball shot? You aren't going on a trip, Bev, you're going on a suicide mission. You're putting yourself at intentional and unnecessary risk for some silly superstition. How about hang-gliding? Parachuting? Will you be kissing the head of a cobra while in Nepal?" Her voice became shrill. "No? Well, now that I've made the suggestion, you might want to hurry and include a snake in your plans."

"I'm aiming for something, that's all. Most of us languish, no goals other than to get in a new bed of petunias before the next rain, or finish wall papering the small bedroom. The bottom line is I have an opportunity to do something wonderful, and the good news is I have the time and money to pull it off. God bless Daddy for insisting that I squirrel away some of each paycheck, and God bless the educators' credit union."

Kimmy and Sara arrived with all the excitement of a jack-in-a box popping open. "Hey Mom. I've brought some of the music tapes you requested."

Wonderful timing. I was glad for the break in tension the girls' arrival provided. We sisters looked up in unison. Lily snapped, "Okay, Bev, I'll see you later." To Kimmy she said, "There's a delicious cake in the kitchen, Honey. Sorry I can't stay now. We'll catch up later." She kissed Kimmy's cheek and stroked little Sara's straight, dark blond hair. "Make sure your grandmom shares that cake, Sara."

I jumped up to catch my sister's arm, "Lily, you're still worried about me. Me too, a little. Look, I'll be back by Valentine's Day. We'll talk about this tomorrow."

My Pioneer Girl granddaughter settled on the floor, singing to Fizz, tangling her fingers in his tail. Feeling every moment with my family was a gift not to be wasted, I involved Kimmy in the packing process.

"Good grief, Mom, you're going to need a larger bag for this heap of tapes."

"Yeah, I might. But, see if you can find my copy of the duet from *The Pearl Fishers*. And I'll need all the Chopin piano concerti that fit in the bag. Do you have the selections of Neil Diamond? Oh, great, here's the Scott Joplin I was afraid I'd lost. Hey Sara, do you have my *Rocky Horror Picture Show* recording?

Sara looked up. "Huh?"

"Mom!" Kimmy disapproved.

"I'm funning with you, Sara, my girl."

*

November galloped into December and Christmas. Despite my excitement and anticipation of my trip, as the departure date loomed closer, my excitement crumbled into mourning.

A week into the new year our usual cast raised our glasses to good health and happiness in 1998, and to my safety during my trip. I was leaving Pine Bluffs and all that I ever loved. I was wrung out from the warring competition between excitement and bereavement in my weary heart.

The good-bye dinner was pork chops, mashed potatoes and sauerkraut, served by Kim on her new Christmas dishes, service for sixteen. Earlier in the day, I'd made an unofficial gift of the dishes to her, saying I was paring back, getting rid of things, and Kimmy and Kevin would have

29

many years of using the holiday dinnerware, to eventually be passed on to Sara.

After a satisfying dinner, I threw my arms around Kimmy's neck where she lingered at the table, and kissed her hard on each cheek. I didn't cry, but only because Lily nudged my foot with her shoe as an eye-opener for me as she carried empty bowls from the table. I sniffed and assisted with clearing away plates and glasses. Sara was sent to the back porch to shake the crumbs from the tablecloth. Kimmy fitted the few leftovers into Tupperware bowls.

I whispered to Sara, "Doing dishes at your house is much nicer now compared to when your Aunt Lily and I were kids at home. We used to fight the whole way through." I started a laugh but had to redirect a tear. "Egads, what's this?" I rubbed my eyes and gave a fake yawn. "Oh, that delicious dinner made me sleepy, girls. Guess I'd better be getting home. Last minute packing and like that."

I gave a cursory good-bye kiss to Kevin. "Best husband in the world, Kev. Keep up the good work," with a cuff to his arm. I scooped Sara off her feet and noisily blew into her neck causing her to scream in joy. I held Kimmy's hand too long and hugged her too lavishly. I looked her in the eye, then petted her head and said, "You've been a great kid. I couldn't have asked for a better daughter."

Kimmy pulled back from my bear hug and protested, "Thanks Mom, but it's not like you're leaving forever."

Realizing I was being a bit too transparent in my affection, I amended, "Although I could have shot you during Algebra II. But you turned out pretty well. You've made me proud."

Kimmy shrugged off my remarks. Her lips rolled in, in a manner of dismissing me, the old girl. "Mom, I, too, was ready to shoot myself during Algebra II."

I left the house, thanking Kimmy again for everything. Everything. She stood in the doorway hugging her arms around her chest. "Don't worry. Aunt Lily and I will be sitting by my phone each Wednesday night at nine waiting for your call. That'll be five, Alaska time, don't forget. Mom, it's way too cold to stand out here saying good-bye. Send lots of postcards. We'll talk. Bon Voyage." Kimmy laughed and closed the door on Aunt Lily, Uncle Stan, and me. I felt the "good-bye forever" didn't seem real. That alone saved me from boo-hooing.

Despite my sad heart, I was proud to have made a proper chance to say good-bye. I'm doing it. I'm saying good-bye and it's a classy thing. Kimmy didn't have any clue about the "last supper."

Stan went home ahead of Lily as she walked beside me to my house. "I told Kimmy if she ever got disgusted with Kevin, she could always come to live with me. Whatta cook."

I answered, "Yeah, what a perfect meal and celebration." Then, seeing Lily's sad face, I elbowed her. "Thanks for keeping the secret. I know Stan will keep the secret too. Can you imagine how the dinner would have gone if Kimmy had known what I was up to? I couldn't have stood it."

"Okay, Bevy, Stan will be here tomorrow at eight-forty-five, on the button. Try to get some sleep."

"Oh yeah, I'm sure to sleep like a log." We stood in the yellow disc of the overhead streetlight and hugged.

31

I was met at the front door by Fizzy. "I wish you understood English, because I want to tell you how much I love you and what a great roommate you've been all these years. I'm happy I'm going on a big vacation, but to tell the truth I'm scared of whatever accident will claim me. But, we can't choose how we go and how much it hurts. I hope dying doesn't take too long."

Despite the inevitable sadness of saying good-bye to family, to Fizz, my home, un-chosen music, uneaten food, I was one hundred percent sure my plan was sensible. I was certain I didn't want my last meal to be a thin, brown, vitamin enriched substance delivered through a nasal feeding tube. I was equally sure I did not want my fading awareness of music as I died, to be obscene lyrics pounding to some dissonant throbbing, raucous, backbeat from the radio of the ambulance that would respond to my motor vehicle accident. Everybody has to go sometime. How about now? This trip was a great thing.

CHAPTER 5

THE FIRST LEG

The next morning Stan called into my kitchen, "Come on Kiddo, we need an early start in case we run into traffic. Car's almost all loaded." He carried the last of my over-packed matching luggage to his car. I looked around my beloved, so clean it was almost unrecognizable kitchen, as neat as a magazine picture. Not a spoon out of order. I bent down to kiss and snuggle Fizz for the last time. I buried my face in his deep fur and told him Aunt Lily would be taking care of him, as Stan rushed in with a facial expression I could not interpret.

"Bev, you're not going to like this. Something you've gotta see. Hurry up." He spun from the kitchen. I gulped and followed. Lily stood at the open trunk of the car with her hands to her mouth. I beheld the largest new bag sprung open at one side seam where unfolding clothes made a successful escape.

"'Feather light and resilient' my foot," I muttered. We three stood, gaping. I joined the pondering. I leaned on my back foot, rubbed my chin and sucked at my teeth. "I'll never forget this moment," I said aloud to the traitor suitcase in the trunk. A few pair of rolled socks lay next to the tire's jack. A long, yellow pullover sleeve stretched to embrace the snow scraper. A sudden suffering of all the possible last minute insecurities swept over me. This is a test. This is nothing we can't handle. Lily pulled me close. I groaned, "Uuuhhh," and turned my back on the colorful tangle of my wayward clothes and looked to Stan. "Do we have time to get to Palmer's Mart?"

Stan suggested, "Here's what we'll do. Lily, get Bev's car from her garage and you two go to Palmer's Hardware. I'll dash home to get one of our bags, in case you can't get a new satchel at the store. It won't be matching, Bev, but it'll be better than nothing. I'll meet you in fifteen minutes. We'll leave Bev's car in Palmer's lot until we come back from the airport. What do you think?" He leaned over with his face a few inches from mine, waiting for my answer.

"Yeah, great."

Stan hopped into his car, backed the half block to his house, and hustled inside to look for the substitute luggage.

Lily shifted her pocketbook on her shoulder. "I'll get your car." She scooped my keys held straight out to her. "Hey, Bev, what's your garage PIN?"

"You have to ask?"

She crossed her eyes. "Oh yeah," and ran off. I dashed inside to get my purse, kissed the cat again, poured the remaining coffee down the drain and rinsed the mug, turned to look at the neat living room to say an all too brief farewell, and locked the back door. My feet felt like concrete. I obeyed the signal of the insistent car horn Lily was leaning on.

She got bossy. "Okay, Bev. I'll leave you at the Palmer's front door then I'll park. You get in there and see what they have. In the meantime, I'll hold a place in the cashier line and will step out when you come through to pay. By the time we're done, Stan will be pulling up. This'll work. Don't worry. You'll get to the airport on time."

I said, "This changes things. All of a sudden you can't wait to get rid of me." Lily reached over and thumped my arm. She leaned forward in the driver's seat as if to urge the car forward. I opened the car window for a long look back at my house and neighborhood disappearing behind January's leafless, angular branches.

She called, "Close the darned window. You're freezing me."

I flattened myself, legs straight out, head thrown back in a posture of resignation. Within ten minutes Lily pulled over to the Palmer's entrance. I jettisoned myself in an inspired leap to the door. I yanked on the door handle and smacked my head into the glass. I stood back and reassured my forehead with a tentative hand, hoping to not discover blood. I rubbed my head as tears of frustration stung my eyes. "What? The store is still closed? Huh? What time is it?" I read "MON-FRI 9 A.M. to …" printed in black block letters and numbers on the sign as I examined my watch. Eight-fifty-nine. "Holy Heaven, I can't friggin' believe this."

A woman holding the hand of a toddler turned from her conversation with other shoppers who stood waiting for nine o'clock. She called, "Not open yet."

I was surprised I hadn't noticed the small cluster of waiting shoppers before. I shifted my weight from the right to left foot like a desperate kid who couldn't wait to get to the bathroom. My worried face was greeted by the cheery, chubby face of old Mrs. Palmer from the other side of the

35

glass door. The plump lady inserted the key, smiled and stood back, admitting me, her first customer.

I exchanged a pleasant greeting and buzzed past the woman. Within a few moments I'd rifled through the luggage choices and paused to consider if I should take yet another matching bag, "feather light and resilient," or to go with a different type of material. My decision was made for me when I couldn't find anything in a sturdier fabric in the size I needed. So, another aubergine "feather light" it was. Good old Lily was standing, talking to the cashier, as so far, there was no one ahead of me checking out. She dutifully stepped aside as I plowed down the aisle creating a speed and collision hazard.

By the time we paid and exited the store, Stan, like the bank-job-get-away-man, was idling at the curb. Lily ripped at the plastic covering the new purchase and shoved me into the back seat with the luggage, old and new. I worked like a robber stuffing money into a bag. Stan drove on.

Back on the road, we had a good laugh at our team work. We jabbered in high energy, excited voices. "I couldn't believe the cashier couldn't get the darned red paper covering on the roll of pennies to crack open. She kept smacking the roll on the lip of the drawer and the dumb thing wouldn't tear open. I thought I'd wet my pants, and all for three cents change." Our nervous laughter filled the car.

At the airport, I hopped from Stan's back seat and tugged at the bags. Lily jumped from the front to help. We sisters ran ahead to the luggage check-in where I thumbed through my passport and ticket one more time. She picked at a small string on my shoulder in a maternal gesture. I gave the ticket agent a vacant smile at her playful remarks about the chances of my luggage going to Alaska. I hoped she was teasing.

In our last hug I laughed as I mock wiped sweat from my brow. "I knew we'd make it. My due date for big things to happen is still weeks away."

"Bev, you scare me. You believe this 2-5-9-8 stuff, don't you?" Lily swung her arms around my neck and cried. I couldn't resist. I returned the hug and bawled louder than my sister.

Stan was breathless when he arrived, witness to our crying and self-conscious laughing. He looked at his watch. He pulled me by my shoulders and looked into my eyes, flooded with tears. "Hey, Bevy-baby, give up a kiss." He pressed his lips to my forehead. I pulled back and fingered my face. "Yikes, that's still sore from whacking my head on the Palmer's front door."

Lily answered, "I'd say so. You should see that lump. At least it's not black and blue — yet.

Others bustled past us as we hugged, laughed, and shot joking insults at each other. Stan took several pictures of us clutching, crying, and kissing. A passing stranger was pressed into service to take a photo of the three of us with our arms circling each other, our fingers digging into each other's shoulders, pulling us closer.

"After that wild beginning, I'm sure the rest of the trip will pale. Look at us; survivors. Well, folks, good-bye, good-bye. Thank you, thank you. Tell everyone I love them and I'll be writing and calling every Wednesday night."

Stan hollered to me as I turned to go, "You didn't think of this on your own, Bev. If you were a rock star, this trip would be called *The Farewell Tour*. All the old groups are doing it."

I shifted my shoulder bag, threw a last kiss, turned and hurried away. My teary eyes watched the polished square floor tiles, distorting into wiggling trapezoids. I was speechless.

Later, buckled into 18-A, both elbows in my lap, I consoled myself with thoughts and replayed fragments of last conversations with my family. I reviewed that Kimmy knew me as either a mean old lady named Mommy, who lost her temper, or the loving lady who sometimes packed a Ring Ding in her lunches.

My mind ran a string of memories like the coming attractions at the movies. I'll never forget how Lily and I laughed ourselves silly when we made bubbles in the tub together as little kids. We tried on Mommy's bras the time she left us with that babysitter who slept the whole time. I'll never forget how scared we were when we drove to a drugstore ten miles away to buy our first box of tampons, and how we skipped school to drive Kenny Baker to the Marine recruiter. My knees knocked in fear of punishment for that trick. Ahhh, my little sister. Wow, I guess she is the person closest to me.

I exhaled, puffing my cheeks, and rubbed the knob on my forehead and winced. "Thank you, Jerry, for inadvertently forcing me to take this trip, this adventure." I was off to the rest of my life. "Good old Stan." I laughed through my words, "He called this trip my 'Farewell Tour.' Oh, how true." I squeezed my eyes shut and muttered my mantra, "This is the right thing to do, this is the right thing to do." I shot a glance to the man in the seat next to me. He was polite or deaf, as he did not react to my talking to myself.

CHAPTER 6

FROST at FAIRBANKS

Swaddled in blankets on the rough-hewn back deck of the Bed and Breakfast, I decided the frigid north wasn't too cold after all. Fairbanks, Alaska's January did not feel much colder than some of Pennsylvania's winters. I scraped my wooden chaise out from under the eaves of the cabin, for a better view of the hoped for Northern Lights display. I blew warm air from my cheeks and watched my breath disperse above bare, distant black tree trunks against the sky's pale background, like so many practice strokes of ink on white paper before calligraphy.

I crossed my feet under the blanket, put my mittened hands under my folded elbows, sat back, and looked up. "Aurora Borealis, aurora, aurora." I rolled the words around in my mouth, "Why didn't I name Kimmy, 'Aurrrorrra?'" I asked myself, stretching out the 'r's. "Because, I had no exposure to people or places other than my own neighbor-hood." I glanced at my blanketed feet and wiggled them. "Well, that was then." I stopped my personal dialogue when I saw I wasn't alone on the deck.

A couple, who appeared to be in their early thirties, were bundled in blankets, cuddled on a wide wooden plank chair. They didn't seem to be the least bit interested in spotting the Aurora. They cooed, and continued kissing,

41

kissing, kissing with me sitting right there. Oh well, Love. To my relief, the cold night, or urgency gave them a good excuse to go inside.

I realized it had been many years since I felt anything like that kind of love for Jerry. He had a way of hurting my feelings even in everyday conversation. He became crabbier and meaner every day. I asked myself if my seeming acquiescence to my married life was to keep up with Lily's apparent happy marriage. Was I afraid to be honest? What would have been the upshot? Nothing. What could I do? Nothing. Maybe his meanness was an illness.

I wonder if Kimmy, the bystander, always present, always observing, has any insights into her father and me. "I wonder if he was frosty to her too. I hope the bastard was good to her when I wasn't present. I guess she and I have to talk about this sometime," I spoke in white puffs to the still sky.

I sat back to consider how exactly a mother broaches that subject? Jerry seemed to tolerate me. No cherishing, no appreciation. How many husbands bring home handcuffs for sex play when he and the wife are in their fifties? I laughed aloud. "What was he thinking?"

A gray cat, with fur thick enough to put this pet in danger of becoming a handsome fur hat, hopped up on to the blankets at my feet. "What a nice surprise! Come here, kitty cat." The cat settled by my hip, also facing the horizon. I laughed. "It's clear you're on the B&B payroll as a guest amenity." I stroked the furry head and whiskers, and joined the cat in searching the hazy sky. "Mr. Pussycat, let me tell you, you'll never regret being nice to your women. I'd laugh, but handcuffs?! I'm sorry my husband died at such a young age, but God, forgive me, I'm so happy to not be married any more. And now that he's been gone for two years, I sometimes look at the occasional couple and wonder if the man's nice to his wife." The cat got up, stretched and walked back into the shadows. I called after him, "Thank you for listening."

My celestial view included a heaven full of unbroken cloud cover. No stars, no moon, no wind, no Aurora Borealis. Despite no light show, I enjoyed the cold night, the silence and the beauty all around me. My mind wandered back to life before Jerry, then, with Jerry when I came to not like him very well, and now, after Jerry. I came to no conclusions, but my privacy of viewing the nighttime white sky with the cold pressed to my face, gave me a feeling of having moved on. If I retold the story, I'd emphasize how, while sitting in Chena Falls, suburb of Fairbanks, Alaska, I'd come to realize I was in a new place. Kimmy would offer an insulting response, "Duhhh." I felt I could go home now and be satisfied with the vacation.

The B&B host had met me at the Fairbanks airport. He was so good looking, my eyes popped open. Unable to hide my pleasant surprise, my face flushed. This was the first chemical reaction I'd had to a man since, I couldn't remember.

He'd introduced himself and loaded my luggage into his old fashioned looking station wagon with wooden exterior features. "I know you've had a long ride today. Welcome to Chena Falls. You've chosen the right B&B. Our view of the night heavens is unobstructed by Fairbanks's ambient night time electrical glow, or trees or power lines." He'd chattered on about today's new three inches of snow, and delivered me to a large private home, with a sign on a white post advertising the B&B. If the same house were in Pennsylvania, it would be a sprawling funeral home. I thought it picturesque, topped off with the new snow.

My jet lag was beginning to feel like heavy velvet across my face. I'd given up on searching for the digits 2,5,9,8 scrawled in Easter egg colors in the heavens above me. I sighed. The day's trip and sleep was beginning to press in on me. I pulled the blanket closer to my neck. The host showed up carrying a small tray, balancing a tall mug of hot chocolate with a peppermint stick poking through the curly, almost frozen, whipped cream cap. He spoke to the blanketed bundle that was me. "I see Jumbles has introduced himself to you. He doesn't discriminate between guests who welcome him and those who are terrified when he wanders from the woods, sometimes with a vole in his mouth."

"I was glad to see him. Gave me someone to talk to." I took a sip of the cocoa then ventured to ask, "Do you think the sky will clear tonight?" I thought he might have laughed to himself at another dumb tourist who didn't know when to come in out of the cold. Mr. Handsome, the strong silent type, shook his head and answered, although his words came from deep in his fur lined hood and were not easily understood. All I could hear was something about, " … and maybe tomorrow night … better visibility … you could never tell … no guarantees and oh, by the way, you have whipped cream on your nose."

Handsome was about my age, had a short, thick beard and sparkling eyes. Under different circumstances I might have downright flirted with him. However, I was pretty sure there was nothing to be gained by saying, "Hi, call me Bev. I'm a recent widow spending my daughter's inheritance, and am seeing the world, until February the 5th when the fates have scheduled me to die. So how are you, Big Boy?" Anyway, I concluded, he's probably gay.

At breakfast on my first morning in Alaska, I was welcomed to the long board covered by a red plaid table-cloth piled with breakfast food. The lovey couple, blue eyed and pink cheeked, were already seated at the family table, awake and laughing. They each raised a cup to me, but went straight back to the absorption of the other. Good for them. They spoke something Nordic, maybe Swedish? Norwegian?

I took in a breath at the scene. The windows were iced with perfect triangles of snow in the southwest corner of each rectangular pane. The sky beyond the glass was a silvery white, melting into a matching horizon. Mr. Handsome stood at the bottom of the table wearing a knee-length apron with bold black letters, "I don't have to lie, I fish in Alaska." The couple clinked their spoons on the coffee cup's sides, as background music to their intimate chatter.

"Oh, this is all so beautiful," I said, directing my compliment to the host, "...your house, furniture, the decorations, the weather, the view, the food, the table. You must be so proud of your lovely place. I can't believe I'm here. And please tell me your name again. I'm sorry I forgot."

"Of course. I'm John Easter. Hence the name, 'The Hutch,' as in the Easter Bunny's hutch, you know, but that's the B&B's name since 1959 when my sister and mother opened. Back in those days these businesses were called, 'Guest Houses.' After I came back from Vietnam I worked with my mom, helping-out, but over the years I found myself in the family biz. Wasn't crazy about the hospitality game at first, but I'm coming to like it. Even starting to bake more of the breads and cakes myself." He leaned to the table and turned the silver tray, loaded with stubby jars of colorful jewels of purple, orange and red preserves. "The jams and jellies are the handiwork of my neighbor down the street. Her name is on the labels, Nancy's Jams. They're great. You'll see."

Ol' John seemed to have a little crush on the jam and jelly lady. Not gay. I nodded and reached for the orange and cranberry preserves to show my good faith in the lady friend's jam making talent. I tasted then gave a genuine smile. "Delicious."

Our host said to the other breakfast guests, "Would you like anything else? I'm embarrassed to say, it's laughable, but, the box of oatmeal I had in the closet turned out to be my container for rubber bands, and a ball of string. I'm so sorry. So, for the oatmeal fans, and I'm one of them, I promise, I'll be buying and serving hearty, hot oatmeal tomorrow morning." He dashed to the kitchen, responding to the binging of the oven's timer.

The Loveys looked into each other's eyes. They didn't seem to care a whit about oatmeal. I'd nodded agreement for tomorrow's menu because my mouth was satisfied with tiny sausages. Boy, when he starts talking, there's no stopping him.

I was impressed with the sumptuous meal set out like a Thanksgiving cornucopia. I broke open a crumbling blueberry muffin and poured a short glass of passion fruit juice. Ummm, great, passion fruit. Tasting the juice with my tongue on the back of my upper front teeth with a tick-tick-tick sound, I concluded, the heck with the passion, it's a fruit. This trip is a good idea, a very good idea.

I stared straight ahead, suddenly feeling conspicuous, alone, and wishing Lily were here to share in this outpost of Chena Falls, boasting a bigger, darker sky, better for observing the Northern Lights. Our host reappeared and offered coffee all around.

"Mr. Easter, can you suggest a dogsled ride for me?"

"Why, yes. My niece and her husband, they're newlyweds, own the company. But they're refurbishing the premises and are renaming the business. I don't know if they're open yet. I'll call Skye."

I nodded.

"I'll have an answer for you later today. After your nap. All East-Coast visitors to Chena Falls collapse on their first full day here, because of the four-hour time change. Trust me, you'll need a nap." I smiled, kept chewing and kept nodding.

"When you do get around to seeing the town, you'll think Chena Falls is an old cowboy town. Tourists take lots of pictures. In the summer of 1954, the movie, *Godfrey's Gold* was filmed here. We're proud of our state, and in particular of Fairbanks and Chena Falls. We have local buses to take you in all directions. Very nice." He spoke with civic pride.

I stuffed the last of my muffin into my mouth while taking in all of the information, thanked my host and licked my finger and thumb. I had several days scheduled in the Fairbanks environs, and was looking forward to the full Alaska experience.

CHAPTER 7

SIGHTSEEING in the FOOD CHAIN

Back in my Pennsylvania bedroom, with clothing choices for Alaska laid out on my bed, I could not have known my new all-weather jacket would be inadequate for Fairbanks. Today, at the B&B, standing over the heap of unpacked clothing, I asked myself how did I overlook winter boots? I'd packed my ankle high hiking boots, perfect for the trip to India, but they were sorely lacking in the warmth and the protection of *real* winter boots? "Oh well," I stepped back, put my hand to my chin in the universal 'I'm thinking' pose. "It'll have to be a couple layers of socks to the rescue, then fall back and punt with shopping," I remarked aloud.

Bobbing my head along with my tape of Scott Joplin's, "The Entertainer," I wriggled into jeans, topping my thin pajama bottoms. My hiking boots were forced on over two pair of socks. My yellow turtleneck shirt was covered by a bulky sweater, topped by my jacket zipped to the chin. I slipped the camera into my coat pocket. Still half singing the final strains of music before leaving my room, I clicked off the tape player, pulled the hood over my stocking cap, tugged on leather gloves, waddled down the stairs and stepped from the warmth of Mr. Easter's vestibule to the snowy steps of the front porch. The cold was so intense the moisture froze in my nostrils. "Colder than a witch's ..." I stopped. "Yeah, mighty cold!"

The silence of the snow assaulted my ears. Mr. Handsome was right. The town reminded me of an old western movie set. Wooden one-and two-story buildings faced each other across a wide street, each side lipped with snow heaped, plank sidewalks. Bolton's Mercantile, home to the Chena Falls Post Office, sat at the end of the block like the proud head of household at the dinner table. I removed a glove, pulled the camera from my pocket, and focused on the swirly gold lettering in the circular advertisement for Bolton's on the large plate glass window. "Ahhh, this is good." Through the lens I couldn't identify people moving about the store, but I saw the pricked up ears of a dog sitting inside the front window. Click. Done.

Noise at last. I heard calling and twisted around to see a German shepherd galloping straight down the middle of the street. I hopped sideways to avoid being knocked over by a happy dog with a heavy cooked ham in its mouth. Chasing the robber was a teen boy, his coat, flapping open as he ran. The parade continued with a woman in a sweater bunched up on her back, clearly pulled on in great haste. A ruffled apron flapped at her waist. The dog was the victor in this race, no question. He disappeared between buildings.

The son called, "Rascal, Rascal. You get back here. Raaascaaalll." He huffed past me, closing in on the corner where the dog had disappeared with a flurry of brown paw pads and kicked up snow. The mother ran with the dimpled fingers of her hand spread on her ample chest, as if to retain

50

the breath in her lungs. I wondered if today's date was *her* four number PIN. Her cheeks were bright red. Her tangled hair blew in unkempt tendrils across her frowning face as she puffed in and out with the effort of her jogging run. I would have liked a snapshot, but decided that although the scene was comical to observe, I was confident the woman, now without a dinner ham, would not see the humor in this particular photo study.

I pivoted to click a picture of the rough-hewn sign nailed to the façade of the Hancock Insurance Company, that announced in large letters, "Sleds and Dogs Must Park Out Back." The storefront was made more picturesque by the plank sidewalk's snow, blown and sculpted into dunes tilting toward the store fronts. As I advanced the film in the camera, the boy came around the side of the church's iron fence, tugging Rascal by his collar. The robber was trotting, pulling his head away from the boy's scolding in a long, unending, railing litany. The dog tipped up his face to his master with every utterance of "Rascal," then blinked and pulled away again at the continued harangue. The mom followed at a distance, taking long strides, not slowed by the snow. She followed the boy and beast, she, hugging the greasy parcel, wrapped in her apron to her bosom. Her hands were redder than before and strands of hair still crossed her face like diagonal ribbon on a package.

"Well, look at that. Mission accomplished," I said aloud. I dared to photograph the three of them, unwitnessed, from behind. The woman was wearing blue, previously fuzzy bedroom slippers when she was called upon to dash from her house.

"Oh, that dog is in for it," I chuckled to myself. "This trip IS a great thing. I wish Lily had come along to see and enjoy this scene."

Slogging past the Methodist church's deserted children's playground, I was once again forced to retrieve my camera to document the four seats of the swing set, hanging still. Each seat held identical six-inch tall, rounded pillows of snow, polished to a smooth glitter by the wind. I stepped into the deeper snow at the side of the playground to get additional photos, but remembered that when in Alaska, to quote Mr. Easter, "If you are fifty feet from the last house, you're in the food chain." Even though I chided myself, of course the bears were all hibernating now, I decided it prudent to not tempt my numbers today.

I returned to the wooden sidewalk watching the town wake up. Four-wheel drive vehicles rumbled down the road, truck tires spinning snow, carving deep tracks, curving and converging to points unseen. Men, clad in various plaids, some with their heads hidden in fur trimmed hoods, hustled into shops, then back to their trucks. No cars, only trucks.

My entrance to Bolton's Mercantile sounded the tinkling bell at the front door. The heat of the store wrapped me in an embrace. "Mmm, nice and warm." I threw back my hood and glanced around. I noticed the dog ears I'd seen through the camera lens were the product of taxidermy. The large grey and white wolf was stilled in a forward lope on the window ledge, one paw lifted, his tongue out. The silent lupine appeared to be watching a stuffed ptarmigan, with its puffed up snowy feathers. The Alaskan state bird watched her inanimate chicks clustered on a fallen log.

Large animal heads disapproved of all shoppers from wooden plaques on the walls. Smaller animals perched among the folded oatmeal sweaters and thick woolen socks, hats and gloves. Pelts of bear and buffalo hung on the knotty pine walls. I felt less like a pioneer woman when I found the shelves of blueberry syrup and Nancy's Jams displayed next to local baked goods. A white taxidermied rabbit sat tall and stared straight at me. A cousin gray rabbit, suspended in a leap was propped by locally made soaps and lotions. All in all, a wonderful store for tourists.

I was willing to bet the store had a genuine potbelly stove. Turning into the first aisle, I grinned at seeing two men, one in a denim apron, enjoying hot coffee poured from the blue enamel pot kept hot on the top of the hot stove. A black stovepipe extended twelve feet straight up through the bas-relief tin ceiling.

"Well, good morning, Mrs. Schuler. Welcome to Chena Falls." He sucked at his pipe and pitched the match into the glowing coals of the predicted potbelly stove. The aproned man introduced himself as Mr. Bolton, the proprietor.

I answered, "What a nice Alaska morning welcome. I guess Mr. Easter called ahead."

He said it was so, and suggested I take my time shopping. He lifted his chin to other tourists meandering through the racks of sweaters and perusing the folded flannel night-gowns. He returned to his interrupted conversation with his friend, whom he called Billy Goat.

After a polite word or two and feeling toasted through-out, I yawned. "I feel as if I've labored through the poppy field. I'd expected to shop, but my jet lag has kicked in, and sleep must be obeyed."

Mr. Bolton said, "Uh-huh, First Day Fog," and backed away to tend to shoppers gathered at the cash register. He called over his shoulder to Billy Goat and me, "How about that dog with the ham in his mouth, leading his sponta-neous procession this morning?"

I answered, "Chena Falls should stage that same show every day for the tourists' entertainment. The dog's smile was worth the trip to Alaska." Waving good-bye over my head and laughing, I pulled my hood over my cap and stepped through the doorway, smiling, remembering Rascal's great get away.

I hustled homeward. Only noon, and the sky was look-ing more like suppertime. I was able to fight off sleep long enough to whip off a short letter to Kimmy. I tucked in a polar bear book mark for Sara. A chatty, informative letter went to Lily and Stan, with promise of more letters to come. I looked at the bed and announced, "I must nap," and sleep I did, until the next morning.

Another crystalline morning and I sprang from bed. Much to my surprise I did something I'd not done in forty years. I dropped to my knees and prayed.

"Dear God, I'm surprised and embarrassed at finding myself on my knees praying like a child but I'm so spiri-tually transported up here in Alaska. I'm no longer feeling alone. I'm surrounded in peace and glorious beauty and I feel I have to say thank you. Thank you, dear Lord. I had to stop and give credit to you for this beauty.

"I want to apologize for what might seem like my superstition about my recurring four numbers. I guess I should have consulted with you before this. The numbers feel like they're directing me, and although I'm somewhat scared by the direction they're taking me, I also have to thank you for this opportunity, this quest. I hope I haven't lost my mind." I dropped my head to my hands, leaned on the bed and cried. "Wow, what was that?" I asked myself, sniffing and wiping at my face, but feeling better for the prayer.

I stood and shivered. "Oooh, it's too cold to be kneeling on the floor in my nightgown." I popped up, put a Chopin piano concerto in the tape player, volume low, and dressed. My heart felt full. "I feel wonderful. I needed to get out of my rut in Pennsylvania." I snapped off the music, scooped up the letters to my family, and was down the steps to a second morning's Chena Falls breakfast.

Mr. Easter served the promised hot oatmeal, topped with brown sugar and raisins. Hot milk steamed from a pitcher. The bounty of food was displayed all about me. The kissing couple was replaced by an Asian family of four. Mr. Handsome dropped two bus schedules at my plate. "One bus gets you to Fairbanks, to the University and points farther west. Fairbanks is a full day's visit with the museums, maybe a show by the young Inuits showing off their physical power and competitive feats. It's a good show. "An eastbound bus will take you to Santa's North Pole. Reindeer wander in Santa's front yard, nibbling the grass. Very popular, especially if you take pictures for your grandchildren.

The town itself is quite delightful, a half-day project, but not to be missed."

I sat back with my mouth open. He bragged on, "All street lights are wrapped in red and white candy cane stripes. I'm proud the town's people decided to incorporate to Santa's town, The North Pole. Everybody in town buys into it. The Chinese restaurant is on Santa Claus Way and the orthopedist's sign advertises, Joel Rabinowitz, M.D., Reindeer Drive. Don't miss it."

The next two days were taken seeing the sights recommended by Mr. Easter. I developed two rolls of film and sent along my captions to the photos. Too much to tell. There's so much beauty and the weather is perfect for staring at the night sky. So far the evening heavens had not shown off the colors that tourists came to this part of the country to experience. But it wasn't yet February.

CHAPTER 8

DOGSLED RIDE

Mr. Easter hailed my arrival at breakfast holding a large serving spoon, recently used to fold the red and green pepper slices over the fat sizzling sausages. "Hi there, Mrs. Schuler. You're confirmed for your dogsled ride, today at two o'clock."

He went on to describe the route from the left turn in front of Bolton's Mercantile, "…keep on going 'til the street narrows to a lane marked by a tall orange flag, attached to a fire hydrant, on the left." He interrupted to add an aside for me, the tourist, "All our fire hydrants are topped with a thin, four-foot pole holding an orange, triangle shaped flag to show above several feet of snow. Anyway, when you see a mailbox shaped like a dog house on the right, that's the place."

"Any chance I'll meet a bear during my walk?"

"Nah, wrong season, but stranger things have happened. Maybe see a moose, maybe a stray husky. I'll walk with you if you're worried."

I braved up and made the sortie on my own, again with camera at the ready. Three hours later, on my victorious return, Mr. Easter met me at the door. "Was the experience tell-worthy? Take any pictures?"

"Oh gosh, yes. I'll be phoning home to give the details, but what a lovely couple and beautiful business they have. I'll send the photos when I get to the end of this roll of film."

"Ready for a hot toddy? Hot chocolate?"

"Oh, yes. Chocolate." I overflowed, "I'm so glad to have someone to talk to. I'm brimming over with stories." I settled at the table where he'd pushed gingerbread cookies in my direction. "Too bad this isn't being recorded, because I'll have to tell the whole story again on my next call home. I had so much fun. Their dogs are so full of personality. Gosh, I miss my pet at home. I needed those dogs.

"Skye and her new husband are so much in love. They approved of everything each other did and said, which is what is so good about being in love, and somewhat short lived." The abruptness of Mr. Easter's knowing laugh gave me reason to suspect he'd been through at least one marriage. "Anyway, I had great fun."

On the following day, a Wednesday, Kimmy reported her curly wall phone wire was stretched to its limit to reach her ear and Lily's. They reported being scrunched together at the kitchen table, their elbows touching as they listened, laughed, and talked to me.

Conversation started with teasing and small talk, confirming everyone was fine, both in Pennsylvania and in Alaska. The phone was passed to Sara, who had stayed up late to talk to her traveling grandmother. I started, "Ohhh, Sara, I wish you were here. It's mighty cold here, though.

"Skye, the beautiful lady who ran the dogsled business asked me to help lay out the dogs' harnesses. She straightened the straps and harnesses in the snow in front of each sled. Sven, her *handsome* husband came around with his big dogs, two at a time, both barking and jumping on their hind legs, pulling and tugging to get hitched to the first sled, anxious to get the party started. Sara, they looked like circus dogs the way they hopped along on their back feet. Sven said, 'Don't worry these are tame dogs.'" I dropped my voice to imitate his deep voice. "'They're loud, but tame. Here, watch me clip Snowy to the harness, then you can clip Chang. Don't worry, I'll check your work.' His wife brought two more dogs, yapping and jumping. We needed two sleds. One was for me, and a larger sled to bring back all the dog food and supplies they were going to buy in the next village.

"I stood in snow up to my shins. 'Brrr.' At last they sat me in a long sled with my feet stretched out in front as if I were a little girl playing 'train' in a cardboard box. Skye covered me up to my neck with a brown furry animal skin. Skye called it a 'gen-u-wine bear pelt.'" I regretted mentioning the pelt in the event Sara could picture too well the process that got the furry blanket from the bear's back to my lap.

"Now, here's the part that surprised me. The whole idea of being a sled dog seems to be to pass the front sled. When the dog team in the back sees the front dog team, the race is on. Tails wag, ears tilt back. The barking is deafening. They seemed to be having so much fun. As soon as we started off, right in front of my unbelieving eyes, smelly canine poo-poos shot out from the running dogs and sank, steaming into the snow, between the tracks and sled runners."

I stopped and listened to the Pennsylvanians' laughter. Sara said, "Uhhh ..." and giggled again. Unseen by my listening public, I flagged away the imaginary odor, inches from my nose. "For an instant the air smelled of fresh doggie-doo, then, as the sled slipped to new snow, the fresh, warm meaty smell was gone, melted deep in the snow forever." We all laughed again.

"After a while you have to trade the front sled to the back, so those poor fellows who were trying to pass, can finally lead. I think the dogs would be happy to carry a thief out of a house with all his stolen booty. But, I don't think the mode of travel will ever catch on with burglars, because there is no silent getaway with a sled of barking dogs."

Sara had had enough and was sent off to bed. I continued with the report. "The young owners of the Old Silver Mine Dogsled Cabin were a magazine-beautiful young couple. They had glowing skin, dewy eyes, Nordic, straight, white blond hair, and pink, pink cheeks. I'll mail their picture along with other photos of the sled ride.

"Skye told me her parents met in Woodstock, then later moved to the big sky of Montana, then to California. They were all nature, sky, and stars sort of people. Well, like a lot of Alaskans, I'm learning. Almost like the Native Americans. She said how glad she was that they named her something as nice as Skye. 'I could have been, Dark Clouds Raining.' She laughed. 'My sisters are Brooke and JANE.'"

Lily asked, "Did her dad later get a job in corporate America and become a Republican?"

I threw my head back in a rollicking response. "You guessed it!"

"Sven's name was Steve, though the kids thought 'Sven' was better for business. They must have had start-up money from their parents, or silver in the old mine, as their digs were modern and quite extensive, including many acres of scrubby pine land, some with hills, some flat.

Lily called, "Go on." I did.

"Alas, all good things come to an end. Back at the cabin, after the dogs' bracing run back and forth to the feed store, there's oh, so much noise. They jump around as they are being rewarded with cut up fish in shallow buckets of water. They sing out and say in full humility, 'Oh it was nothing at all ... I enjoyed it ... No, no, thank YOU for choosing me ... See? I can jump higher than that other dog over there.' Their tails wagged and slapped into each other's faces. 'Hey, hey, some more fish over here, Hey, ME, here, over here, me, ME, give me a little more, Hey, what am I, chopped liver? Thank you, thank you.' An asthmatic would die right on the spot from the cloud of dog fur and dander. Even the dogs have the Alaskan spirit. I wish you were here to share this trip. If I think of anything else, I'll write it in the next letter."

My next letter had the list of remembered dog's names: Choko, Snowy, Mama Bear, Freckles, Misha, Arrow, and Ethel and another six, sat outside Sven's barn. I wrote about the individual flat topped dog houses each with a chain attached to the dog's collar. The dogs sat on their roofs, supervising and yipping opinion, sure to not miss any activity by being inside the house.

I took photos of the leather harnesses and ropes hung on pegs by each dog's name painted on the barn wall. Work benches held sled runners, nails, and various pieces

61

of hardware, waiting for repair in the barn. Oh, so beautiful. Thank you 2-5-9-8 for giving me this opportunity.

*

On day five of Alaska, I faced up to returning to Bolton's Mercantile for shopping for those at home. I chose rose petal pink soaps and creamy white beeswax lotion, then loaded three bottles of blueberry syrup into the basket. I found my way to the Alaskan gemstone counter and again I could not resist original and unique gifts for Kimmy and Lily. I hoisted the crystal clusters of amethyst and clear rhomboids of mica. "Oh, how does one decide?" I asked myself, weighing the crystals in my palms.

Mr. Bolton rang up the purchases, again offering to mail the packages. I promised to return after I'd sorted through the gifts and added notes to each. I'd also decided to keep one of the soaps and a silky green scarf. I re-zipped, pulled my cap to my ears, and called good-bye. The wind had picked up. I tied my hood close to my chin and rearranged my bulky bag of gifts and stepped outside.

Ka-pow! A stray dog, loping past the mercantile, was lifted from his feet and pounded into my low legs. "Ow!" I leaned down to reassure my shins, in an involuntary reaction to the blow to my legs. My hands came down on the dog's back. He whimpered and crumpled at my feet. "Oooh, poor..."

Ka-pow! A second shot sounded. I couldn't find the source of the loud report. I was spun around and was thrown into the Bolton Mercantile window. I cried in pain. The bullet seared my left arm slamming me backwards through the broken window, split by the same bullet. I was hit by a blizzard of shattering glass. I landed on my back against the firm ribs of the stuffed wolf. The powdered glass blew into the feathers of the family of ptarmigans on a log, and dusted my coat, the fur of my hood, my squeezed shut eyes, and forehead. I flung my arms out, dropping the packages across my lap. I lay still, not knowing how I came to be propelled through the store's window display. My head and upper body lay among the wolf and ptarmigans. My legs dangled outside, a few inches above the wooden, plank sidewalk.

Ka-pow! A third shot hit the frame above the now empty window. An eight-inch delta shaped slice of plate glass hung above my waist and upper legs. I watched in disbelief as, after a single second of seeming to hold its breath, the dagger of glass relinquished its hold, then surrendered in a storm of splinters on and around me.

The bagged gift of amethysts and mica and the rounded bottles of blueberry syrup that lay across my middle deflected the glass, that then splashed across the stuffed wolf and game birds. The syrup bled into the shopping bag and across my hips and legs and into the window display. Raw glass nicked my forehead and my squeezed shut eyelids.

Voices erupted. Shouts filled the air. People in parkas and store owners in shirt sleeves dashed from trucks and shops. Mr. Bolton shoved his arms into his coat as he grabbed for me. "Ma'am, are you all right?" He turned and called, "Billy, hurry up and call the ambulance."

63

CHAPTER 9

SHOPPING and SHOT

I winced, aware of the searing pain in my arm, and wondered how I'd come to be lying on my back, and *inside* Bolton's front window. My face was frosted with glass collected between my lips, across my face and powdered in the fur trim of my hood.

I spat grainy glass from my lips. Mr. Bolton dusted my face with a glove he'd pulled from his jacket pocket, and helped me to sit, asking if I were all right. He surveyed the overhead frame of the window. No further glass shards threatened to separate from the window frame.

Drifting up from my temporary unconsciousness, I became aware of my uninvited, undeserved, off schedule accident. I was thankful I'd tied the parka hood so close to my eyes and chin two seconds before stepping into harm's way.

Mr. Bolton, first to my side, called in a throaty, panicky voice, "Thank God you decided to carry your purchases. The heap of the rounded bottles and gemstones broke the fall of that overhead pane of glass."

I mumbled a disoriented answer. I didn't remember the package I'd carried.

He called, "The arm of your coat has a tear. Oh, there's blood. You're hit! Billy, she's been shot! Be sure that ambulance is on its way."

The emergency van, with me in the rear, wailed its way to the clinic in Chena Falls. Out of the ambulance, and into a wheelchair, I was rolled to a triage nurse where I was evaluated and a temporary bandage was applied to my arm. Then, into a typical, curtained examination room for me, the ER's third patient that morning.

I was propped up and given an outdated movie magazine to peruse while I waited for the next thing. My attention was caught by Mr. Bolton poking his head around the cubicle's striped curtain, wiggling his fingers in a self-conscious wave, requesting admittance. He crept in and stood over me in a late, protective posture. I felt weak, but was glad to see a familiar face.

"Thank you, Mr. Bolton for staying with me. I'll be okay now if you want to get back to your business."

He answered, "I'll hang around until the doc comes in. I have ol' Billy Goat keeping the shop. Let's consider me as your Uncle Bolty for today since only family is allowed back here. Besides, I thought you might like to hear what happened to you, since you up and fainted like a girl from the lower forty-eight, just because you got shot." He winked and tapped my injured arm, dangerously close to the bandage.

I winced and leaned backwards. "Whoooa." I inhaled and wasn't able to mask the hurt. "I'll bet a good ole strapping Alaskan woman would have punched you back for that." I took in a deep breath and invited his story. "Let's hear it, Unk."

He started, bushy eyebrows high, his hands swinging in swirling flourishes. "I heard the gunshots and saw you being blown through my window all at the same time. People on the street hollered. A little boy about this high was bawling to beat the band as his bigger brother yanked him by his coat collar and swore at him. He kept calling the little brother a, pardon me, Mrs. Schuler, he called him a little fff, I can't say it," he shook his head and apologized.

"Anyway, the big kid yanked his brother's collar, half beating him as he kept swearing and saying his dad was going to kill them both. Their father showed up along with the neighbors, store owners, and patrons, running from trucks and shops. You're a celebrity!"

As Mr. Bolton told his story, a tall man, looking like all other Alaskan men, in a plaid shirt and open parka, pushed the curtain back and walked into my cubicle. Another uncle? He stood in front of me and my raconteur, flanked by two, black-haired boys. He had my attention. He clapped a beefy hand on the shoulder of each of his sons. "Ma'am, my name is Pug St. James and these are my sons, Anthony, ten, and Sammy, who turned six last week. I believe my boys have something to say to you." With this he shoved forward the quaking older boy.

Anthony looked to his scowling dad, then to the floor as he said, "I, uh, was, uh, supposed to watch Sammy while Dad went into the store. But I, uh, turned on the radio, and, uh ..."

His father thumped Anthony's back. The child continued, "I'm not allowed to turn the radio on. It wastes batteries, and that's bad in Alaska when you never know when you need all the battery power you can get." He was quoting an oft heard platitude.

His dad grumbled, "This isn't about the batteries, Anthony."

"I heard a rifle shot. When I looked up Sammy was gone from the back seat, and so was Dad's rifle from the gun rack in the truck. I heard another shot and ran, looking for Sammy. There he was, lying in the snow on his back. The rifle knocked 'im off his feet. I pulled 'im up, and he cried and picked up the rifle that was too heavy for him, and somehow another shot flew out. But he didn't kill nobody. Well, maybe the old dog got it." With the last sentence he collapsed into his dad's side and bawled.

Mr. St. James pushed little Sammy forward. "Go ahead Sammy, get it over with. This is the lady you shot. What do you have to say? Say the right thing Sammy. This isn't over."

The trembling child looked at me sitting with my hands clasped between my knees. My eyes were wide, my lips bitten in a tight line. I had to forgive the tiny boy as he shifted his weight and inched back to the security of his dad's leg behind him. He wavered and bawled. His nose ran and tears shot from his eyes. Sammy cried out, "The rifle smoked. It smoked." The remainder of his confession was unintelligible.

Anthony recovered. "The barrel of the rifle was hot so the cold snow made it smoke. It scared 'im."

Mr. St. James yanked Sammy's jacket, "That's enough." He looked into my face, "Mrs., I'll replace your jacket, but that's all I can do."

A nurse appeared at the cubicle. She frowned at the contrite father and two underage children, as she bossed, "How did you get back here? This is a private patient area. You and those children must wait in the waiting room. Please." All eyebrows raised at the curt order.

Mr. St. James turned to leave but finished his speech. "And, I'll discipline the boys, of course. This kind of thing will never happen again. I guarantee." He grabbed each boys' hood and turned to leave, looking from the rear as if he were carrying two short tents with legs and feet.

I looked at Mr. Bolton. "Wow. Are those kids going to be safe?"

"Sure they are. This is a tough town and they need to be taught their lesson. They'll get over it."

I asked, "Did the dad say his first name was "Pug?"

"Yeah, maybe he was 'pugnacious' as a kid." Mr. Bolton laughed. "He's not the only 'Pug' around here. And, the old dog isn't dead. He was alive when the owner of Hancock Insurance picked him up and hurried him over to the vet while you were being loaded into the ambulance. We value our sled dogs."

"Pennsylvania girls care about dogs too, and hope they survive." As I shook my head and said, "Poor innocent dog," a doctor, followed by an assistant carrying a suturing kit entered. Uncle Bolty recognized his cue. He turned to me, "I'll drive you back to town when you're ready." He directed his next comment over his shoulder to the doctor as he left the cubicle, "Now, don't make her cry. She's a famous, visiting dignitary from Pennsylvania." With that he returned to the waiting room.

Back in the B&B, later in the afternoon, I rolled from my pain medicine enhanced nap, awakened by Mr. Easter tapping on my door. He was delivering a large basket from Bolton's Mercantile. I sat up with painful effort, unwrapped and examined bottles of replacement jams, soap and blueberry syrup. A bright purple sweat suit to compensate for the ruined slacks now stained in canine blood and syrup lay in the bottom of the basket. An olive green canvas jacket with a hood, zippers, and pockets, was folded in a gift box with the note, "Very sorry, Mrs., From the St. James Family."

John Easter's sympathies were evident in the bouquet of dried and straw flowers delivered to my room. I fingered through the replaced gifts, and flopped face down into my pillow and cried, "Oh, how I miss Sara. The bigger boy, Anthony St. James, was Sara's age. To think I may never see her again. Ohhh, how selfish of me to take this trip." My crying evolved into a restorative nap.

When awake, and seeing the sky was still pink before the night closed in, I dressed in my many layers, pulled on my new olive green jacket, and walked to the corner to The Pie Hole for supper. I carried my letter writing supplies and spread them on the table.

Dear Lily, My goodness, this charming town of Chena Falls is full of local color. Today a little boy managed to snare his dad's rifle and accidentally winged a dog. Oh what a fuss. But, maybe these things happen every day, because everyone has guns and rifles.

I wondered if I'd said too much. Nah. If all these accidents were happening before my "date," I wondered what whopper awaited me on 2-5-98. Back to the letter I added, *Anyway, I'm fine and am looking forward to sighting the aurora. Never say die. Not yet.*

CHAPTER 10

THE AURORA

On day six of beautiful snowy nights without a sighting of the Northern Lights, I faced up to returning to the Fairbanks suburbs. I muttered, "… if this city had any idea how much this trip is costing me, and that I'm never coming back, they'd give me one bang-up display of fireworks, I'm sure."

John Easter corralled me with a change of plans for my evening departure. He carried an unopened jar of palm hearts he'd been trying to force open. "It seems," he said, "your plane is unable to leave Fairbanks tonight, some kind of mechanical problem. So, knowing that Fairbanks is the start of your vacation, and all other flights depend on you leaving our fair city on time, I have spoken to the pilot of the mail plane that leaves Chena Falls every night at six. He is willing to take you to Anchorage, and will be taking a few other passengers who also need to get to connecting flights."

I stood with an open mouth listening to this seeming impossible turn of events. I recalled Lily's voice and words, "Beverly, you never know what awful things could happen away from home. Who'd you call?"

John continued, "The cost of the flight will be negotiated by the pilots, no change in price to you. You'll fly in a

71

plane hired out for the mail delivery, and it's legal and safe enough. How about it?" He gave me a second to make up my mind as he finished his proposal. He tapped his thumb on the palm heart's lid. "Mail plane leaves in two hours."

Why not? "So, sure. That's great. I appreciate it." I sang in my head, "Hah-hah Lily, you were trumped." I dashed up the stairs. I'd be changing flights in Anchorage in a few hours. Next stop, Russia.

Ol' John Easter, a man of action, piled my pyramid of purple bags into his long station wagon, and in sprays of snow spinning from the tires, we were off to a Chena Falls airstrip in a field, close to the town. Mr. Easter and I looked each other in the eyes, and hugged good-bye and I was off to Anchorage and air connections going west. His memory of me would be a fat, blue, gauzy bag filled with M&Ms, left on the bureau with a thank you note for his kindnesses.

*

The pilot helped me to climb into a small, yellow, wooden plane. He explained the plane was called a widgeon. It predates the Second World War.

"Good grief, I'm so embarrassed. This is the opposite of birth," I blurted in a laugh as I entered the body of the fuselage through the underside of the tail section. The plane allowed seats, single file next to each wall and window. I hoped the two men already seated across from each other hadn't heard my entrance remark as they were laughing and comparing their successes from their recent fishing expedition. Each man was costumed in the standard Alaska fare and tie up boots and usual jeans. One man was flourishing his stocking cap about as he laughed and reminisced, while the other's cap covered his bushy hair.

I whispered to myself, "I swear, more Paul Bunyans."

Both men had down filled vests and jackets thrown at their feet and each had a picnic cooler stowed behind the rigid wire mesh wall that kept the mail bags and parcels secured and apart from the few passenger seats. The men held a jolly exchange about their fish, ice packed and stacked to the brim of their coolers. As I ducked into a seat behind Bachelor Number Two, a third, hearty man with gold chunk jewelry on his fingers climbed through the rear end calling hello to all. Nodding and smiling, he strapped his large bellied self, with great effort, into the seat across from me.

The yellow mail plane circled to the end of the runway as we four pioneers stuffed yellow protective sponge cones into our ears. Two pickup trucks with headlights aimed at the plane's path provided the do-it-yourself runway lights. The brave plane lifted into the sky with a sudden and steep tipping of the wings as it left the ground. I thought this a quaint signal of good-bye, like in the movies. The considerable noise of the widgeon's engines forced us to end our fruitless effort at conversation.

The whole Fairbanks vacation had been wonderful, with the obvious exception of me being shot in the arm, and suffering through the St. James kids' confessions. I sat back, and rubbed my sutures, while putting the Alaskan trip into perspective. I was pulled from my reverie by the men looking through their windows pointing and mouthing, "Ohhh"s and "Look at that's."

The Northern Lights were on the other side of my window, nose level, doing their electrical dance, and not a minute too soon. What had started as a sad good-bye to a town that failed to produce a sighting of the Aurora Borealis, was now providing a swirl of colorful light. I laughed out loud, and clapped my gloved hands at being engulfed in the show. The display came early in the night as thick shots of pale rainbow blew apart, curling and waving, and disappeared like trailing ribbon caught in a breeze. I was rewarded with banners of three flavors of white: bright, dazzling, and pale smoky white, as the light streams wrapped and unwrapped their shimmering and undulating stripes.

The aurora was reflected on the rounded cheeks of the smiling men, and on the glasses of Bachelor Number Two as he watched the lights. I was speechless. I grabbed for my camera and snapped away to the end of the roll of film.

The tiny stars in the black sky sat back and enjoyed the spectacle, a show they had seen many times before. After fifteen minutes and the continued south-western trajectory of the plane, there was unending black sky to be seen. The aurora was either played out or the plane outstripped the lights' westward journey. The celestial celebration ended, but what an event it had been. Rather than exclaiming to each other, we passengers sat in a stunned and private silence at nature's extravaganza.

I pressed my head against the, too old to be pressurized window pane, and whispered a short prayer into the darkness, "God, I don't want to die. I want to see more of your starry skies. I want to kiss my granddaughter and daughter again. I want to laugh again the way I laughed with those sled dogs. I want to continue to marvel at life every day. I want more music, more chocolate, more time, maybe even a chance to dance slow and close to a man again, maybe even kiss him. And thank you for the safe and wonderful life I've had."

Within an hour the city of Anchorage lit up the sky and the yellow widgeon headed into a landing. Outside the plane, the pilot handed the luggage to his departing passengers. We recounted the thrill of seeing the Northern Lights. For him, the aurora was a frequent phenomenon. He was more interested in telling us that in his takeoff from Chena Falls, he had to tip the wings to avoid hitting a moose, who'd wandered onto the short runway. The huge animal must have been deaf, or nearsighted, or was suicidal. I thought the wing tipping had been a nice touch, a quaint good-bye.

CHAPTER 11

RUSSIA and the
PECTOPAH

I had to admit to an unexplained spooky fear of being alone in Russia. I stroked my stitched up left upper arm and divined that my unsettled feeling must have been born of old movies, plus my readings of Solzhenitsyn's first hand reports of Soviet Russia. I lugged my bags to the bus transfer point after surviving my somewhat frosty interaction with the uniformed visa and passport people. They, somewhat low on the congeniality score, were the only negative so far, but I'd been in the country for a mere twenty-five minutes.

As I tromped from the plane with the other weary tourists, I belatedly asked myself why I'd wanted to come to Russia. I'm here and I know I'll love it. I counted off reasons with each step. Left - "Russian ballet." Right - "Nesting dolls," Left - "Nabokov." Right - "Rimsky-Korsakov." I bobbed my head from side to side in the naming game, continuing with each step in the long corridor: "Shostakovich ... Nyet and Da ... Tchaikovsky ... men named Ivan ... Vladiamir ... babka ... Prokofiev ... Nureyev ...borscht ... vodka ... Czars and czarinas. Hooray — I'm here!"

The Saint Petersburg airport was stark, but not scarier than other airports I'd seen. Jerry and I'd changed planes in Mexico on our honeymoon. I'd been to England and Rome in high school, and had seen a few U.S. cities' airports. Nope, this wasn't worse. A quick look around and I was assured I looked like the gentry, all coated and scarfed. To be an invisible tourist, however, I'd need a fur hat.

The first visual jolts to remind me I was indeed in a foreign land were the street and shop signs with upside down 'V's and backwards 'N's. A vendor moving among the fresh bunch of tourists was hawking Russian postcards. He was a middle - aged man, tall and good looking, showing no physical or mental defect, but in shabby clothes. I concluded maybe he was a deposed prince. He had an altogether wrong look for one in such a menial job.

I boarded a bus sent from the hotels to gather up and deposit the tourists at their proper destinations. A plush conveyance, I'd have to rethink my preconceived thoughts of Russia. The buildings were as I'd seen in photos and in movies; gray, ornate facades behind loops and loops of electrical wires overhead. Unfamiliar small cars, looking more like be-wheeled turtles, bugged around on the slushy streets. The hotel was the fourth stop. My cursory scan of the passengers was halted by blue eyes in the shadow of a gray fedora. His steady gaze made me think he was someone who'd recognized me. A tentative smile started until I remembered that I knew not one soul in all of Russia. I averted my eyes, surmising he was yet another man in another country doing what men do. No language necessary.

"Gosh, if someone dropped me into this spot, I'd guess I'm in Russia." Gloves pulled from my hands, I wrote in my little notebook, *I feel I'm in a scene from a black and white movie. Anyway, lucky me, I'm here.* As I wrote, the woman in the seat next to me moved to the back of the bus. I wondered if maybe I shouldn't be writing in public. The hotel's address is 2589 Pushkin Grand. My eyebrows went up. A half-smile pulled at one cheek.

Into my room, I shot my hand through the folded clothing to retrieve my electrical adapter so I could listen to my tape player. Due to the gloominess of my mood, and the day, Neil Diamond was my choice for keeping me company. I played, "Coming to America," getting reassurance that people fled to America then sang about it.

I settled at my Russian desk and wrote: *The lobby was meant to walk through: in or out. No loitering here. All signs in the hotel are in Cyrillic and English. That's more than fair. No one is going to see a Russian sign in any hotel lobby in Philadelphia, or New Jersey, or at any of our train stations.*

I stopped writing to wonder about the man in the gray fedora and his long trench coat. My creative brain told me he looked as if he were in a required costume for the average spy from the 1960s. Maybe he was police, watching everybody. Maybe he was a masher. Maybe he was some poor Josef Schmo who lived near this hotel. "Is my paranoia beginning to show? I'm overreacting, a victim of the scary spy movies." I found speaking aloud to be a strange and welcome comfort.

I returned to the lobby to pay, in rubles, for an English spoken tour of the city on the following morning. Back to my room I paged through my *Quick Translation* language folder. '*Remember, the 'P' in Russia, has the 'R' sound in English.*' Great, I had been looking forward to going to the *Pectopah*, but it turns out I'm going to an ordinary old restaurant. Maybe I'll name my next kid *Pectopah*.

I made my way down twisty hotel corridors and arrived at the *Pectopah* and was seated at a table for two. No sooner had I placed my purse on the chair next to me than I was approached by two young people in spiky, iridescent, pinky-red hair, their necks ringed in large dog collars of black leather with silver studs and buckles. Each had a few facial piercings.

"Hello, Missus." The young woman smiled showing straight white teeth and introduced herself as Zelda. I watched the young woman, thinking some nice German mother was worried about her pretty young daughter who took off with the wrong dude and was living in Russia. Zelda had long, dark eyelashes and heavy eyeliner. Her bare arms poked from a furry black vest. Redundant at her dog collar, was a blue, home-knitted scarf hanging past her flat buttocks.

Her partner, a lanky beau, not much different in garment, was introduced as Helmut. He managed a sparse beard. Helmut was likewise underdressed for the weather. His bare chest was covered with a black leather vest over pale, white skin.

Zelda spoke, "Missus, we are having a party in the Ratskeller of this hotel. Many friends are coming. No drugs, don't worry. We sing. Helmut does the discs. Small ... fee? Charge? ... klein ... pay at door. Tonight." She smiled again.

I was intrigued by this handsome couple, looking like escapees from a recent dystopian movie. Both looked healthy and were good looking. The girl struggled with

English, but her German tongue also had to manage Russian. Quite the challenge. I confessed to myself that Zelda's English was okay, better than I could do in another language. Helmut teased about her awkward speech in his fluent English. He flourished a business card to me. Zelda blushed. She had Shirley Temple dimples at the corners of her lower lip. I nodded and accepted a black business card with *Ratskeller* written in red. Truth was proving, indeed, to be stranger than fiction. I decided that keeping company with a couple of beat-biker singers would beef up the next Wednesday's call home. The beat kids looked harmless. "I'll be there."

Zelda and Helmut turned to a table of three well-bellied men, all in business suits, and gave the same speech, and likewise, handed a like card to each. I settled down to order my Russian dinner, choosing from the menu with English translations next to color photos. I chose local specialties: cabbage soup followed by shrimp with a potato puff, and caviar on thin toast.

"Ach, Russian sturgeon. Can't miss out," I said to my menu. After a satisfactory dinner of Russian fare, I returned to my room for another short nap. The jet travel was taking its toll, demanding payback.

Awake at eleven p.m., I considered rolling over and returning to sleep, but the Ruskie equivalent of Montezuma's revenge spurred me from bed. I directed my resolve to the tired looking woman in the mirror, "Well, I'm up, so I might as well go boogie with the youth of Russia."

I dressed in black everything down to my flat shoes. I wore dangly silver oval earrings, then tied a new green and red fringed scarf around my waist and hips. "I hope I look dissolute enough for the occasion. Kimmy would disown me." I held my coat and key, and told the darkened room, "Okay, it's off to a Saint Petersburg, Ratskeller night." A second thought seeped into my conscious, "I hope I don't get arrested or shot for being in a pot-smoky dive. Wait, I've already been shot. So, all that and heavy metal music should be fun. Ah, but such an interesting obituary!" I threw my coat over my shoulders, locked my room and headed to the elevators. Kimmy would enjoy this outing.

I marched through the empty lobby and into the cold, black night, lit with neon signs and five-foot tall, spicy underwear advertisements. I was surprised by Russia's racy, lacy, body exposure compared to the prissier ads in liberal USA. More fodder for the phone call home. I kept my head down and followed two young women, whose elbows were locked together while they walked in step. The two were in short black coats, and tall black boots, hurrying to the same night's entertainment. The line of twenty-somethings snaked around the corner to the back end of the hotel. I joined the line and tried to not look like a senior chaperone to the young people. I relaxed, hands deep in my pockets, and leaned back on one foot to affect cool insouciance. I looked up to the starry sky and wished I'd brought my sunglasses. A young fellow four couples forward was wearing his sunglasses. My belly growled. I frowned and patted my stomach. "Down boy," I said to my coat.

Doors opened. Couples of all variety moved into the dark room with cheerful greetings and bantering. Revolving lights hung from the ceiling, slinging colors across the dark room where tables for four or eight were pushed together. The youth signaled for drinks and reached for karaoke books. Karaoke? What a surprise.

The tall man on the stage behind the turntable and disc set up was Helmut. Good work, Helmut. His pink hair was covered in formidable earphones. His leather vest was replaced by a silky, turquoise, tux's vest, still devoid of shirt, although as formal wear custom dictated, he wore a matching bowtie against his bare throat. Cute.

Topped off with a smoke gray, Russian spy fedora, dangerously tipped over one eyebrow, Zelda moved back and forth across the stage, moving the mics, making sense of the power cords, reaching up to adjust lights. She saw me, grinned, and waved from the stage like a kid waving a "Hi Mommy" greeting. I returned the wave and ordered a vodka. 'When in Rome,' and settled back to enjoy the show.

I was no stranger to karaoke. I'd gone out singing with Kimmy and some of her girlfriends for the occasional birthday, and for one friend's divorce in Pennsylvania. I smiled at the fiftyish man who was handing out the karaoke books to the eager flock. The tall fellow, dressed in a tweed jacket, took my smile as an invitation and settled himself next to me with a vodka in each hand. He leaned in, swinging his arm behind my chair. Smooth. I didn't open the karaoke book, knowing I couldn't read Cyrillic titles. When I waved away the book, the man directed a Russian question to me. I excused myself in English. He pushed a short glass filled to the lip toward me and introduced himself as Rrrrobbie, rolling his 'r's. He spoke in tolerable English, as the music blotted out his words.

The kids sang in their mother tongue, then in English, then pulled out one French song that had many 'La-la-la's in it. The audience applauded and the brave singers sang again and again. Helmut bounced around in his station, leaning, rolling and enjoying each selection. Zelda took up the mic and sang, "I Am Woman Hear Me Roar," in English. The dance floor was filled with the fair sex swinging their arms over their heads, hugging each other, and kicking off their boots. When the song ended, the sisterhood stood in the center of the floor, grinning, laughing, and clapping at the good time.

"You must get up and sing. Show Rrrrussia what talent looks like," Robbie called. A magnanimous fellow, he offered to sing along.

I called over the music, twice, same sentence, "You're persuasive, but I can't sing."

Robbie, not dissuaded, cupped his hand behind his ear and over the notes of "Hotel California," called, the Russian, "What?" I yelled another excuse over the loud music, my English louder than before. He reached for my hand and in the single second of silence before Helmut announced the next singer, I broadcast to the whole congregation, sober and not, "I'm fifty-five-years old and waaay too old to get up in front of all these kids."

One second of silence, two seconds, then boisterous laughter was followed by thunderous applause and foot stomping. I was cooked, and had no choice but to get up and sing with Robbie the Russian, as soon as the tiny imitation of Edith Piaf finished her soulful rendition. Robbie pulled me up through the inky darkness, into the white spotlight.

Iridescent strobes blitzed the room. Red, gold, and green faces came and went in the jittery lighting pattern.

My head felt disembodied. I was feeling faint, but Robbie's steady grip of my gunshot, stitched upper arm kept me upright. I winced, but muscled through. He called to Helmut to play Sonny & Cher's, "I Got You Babe," a tried and true crowd pleaser. The music started. I grasped my mic, and hip to hip, swayed with the music. I dared another smile right up to Robbie's face. The old folks was a 'groovin'. When we got to the line where the man sings, "... put you little hand in mine," he released his hold on my waist and held my hand above our heads for all to see. Without his support I stumbled backwards. Perhaps, he suspected I couldn't hold my liquor, but I was thinking this was a problem of shrimp dinner gone wrong, and before long, the problem would resolve itself, and not in a socially acceptable way.

When he got to, "I got you to walk with me," he turned, smiled at me and bobbing his head in time to the music, indicated with his eyebrows it was my turn to answer, "I got you to talk with me." But, alas, my eyes bulged as my mouth filled with regurgitated seafood dinner. I shoved my microphone to Robbie and felt my cheeks threaten to give way. I staggered behind a six-foot tall, cut-out cardboard dancing bear wearing a clown's ruffled collar, and holding up a sign for a *dunkle Bier.* I backed out of the spotlight, fanning my face with my hand. The savvy barkeep handed me a wet tea towel and plastic bucket, not yet emptied of ice chips. To the tune of, "I got you to hold you tight," I threw-up

The section of the audience who saw me said an, unnecessary need to translate, "Eeewww." Those not witness to the event continued singing and concluded in legato, "I got you Baaabe." Applause, applause, applause for Robbie, as I was no longer in evidence to be regaled.

Robbie helped me get back to the hotel. I kept saying, " ... the shrimp ... the seafood ...," for some reason, feeling it necessary to disclaim the Russian vodka as the reason for the gastric display. Good news was Robbie left as soon as he got me back to my hotel room. I pitched my purse to the bed and dove into the bathroom. I spent the night on the cold, tile floor, next to the efficient toilet, designed to deliver full or half flushes, this feature not mentioned in any of the postcards. Draped in large, white hotel towels, with my teeth chattering, I shivered, and repented over the Russian dinner. Good God, it never occurred to me, my demise might be food poisoning. Wrong date.

Kimmy would accuse, "Moth-Er. You were drugged." How like a hackneyed plot. I doubted it, but the thought gave me pause. Had I been drugged? Had Robbie slipped me a mickey? Heck, I was sort of hoping he'd be the guy I'd have a close dance with. My head spun, spiraling my rational thoughts. Nah, I'm not a twenty-three-year old sex goddess, promising hot money on the white slave trade. I laughed at my ridiculousness. It was the damned shrimp. Even thinking the word, 'shrimp' made me burp. And to top it off, the stitches in my darned gunshot arm throbbed. Damn.

On my Wednesday night's call to Kimmy and Lily I told of my moment of disgrace in Saint Petersburg, Russia's hot

Ratskeller, handsome Robbie, and tainted shrimp, all illuminated by strobe lights. I described the cardboard bear I'd hidden behind, leaving out my temporary worry of being part of a white slavery scheme and the possibility of being given a "mickey."

Kimmy was on the other end of the phone connection laughing through her words, "Oh, no, Mom. Don't tell me. Oh, no."

Lily was giggling in the background. Kevin was stage whispering, "What? What's so funny?"

Kimmy went on, "I can't believe this, Mom, no, no."

I congratulated myself on embarrassing my daughter despite that we were separated by an entire ocean. Another parenting success.

CHAPTER 12

BORSCHT and NEW BOOTS

Next morning, I was as pale as the bathroom sink, and not much warmer. Looking at my reflection I said, "Ah, so zombies DO exist." I brushed my teeth and hot showered and with some swearing, saw I'd missed the ten a.m. English bus tour around town. Into clothes and back to the empty lobby, I rescheduled a later bus tour. Back to lounging in my room, waiting for the trip, I erupted into laughter from time to time, remembering how I'd yelled, "I'm fifty-five," in the one second of dead silence, and at the fun I'd had singing and dancing with tall and adequate Robbie, who rolled his 'R's. Forget Kimmy's embarrassment, Jerry would have disowned me. Good. I'd be remembered as the old American lady who couldn't hold her vodka. I wished the best for pink-haired Helmut and beautiful dimpled Zelda. They were kind and generous to me; the youth of tomorrow.

A white sky greeted Saint Petersburg on January 26th. I scanned the sky and concluded, a sky like this in Pennsylvania means snow. "Let's see how things play out here in Russia." I walked through the lobby and boarded the large bus, took a window seat and was soon joined by a group of assorted tourists, all rosy cheeked and bright eyed.

I was impressed the tour was conducted in English for the group, that included fourteen Asians, who showed excitement at being there.

A knot of locals sat too far away for me to hear their language, but my money said this was not a group from Detroit. The men, heavily coated, all stocky and in fur hats or flat smooth ear muffs entered the bus. When I next spoke to Kimmy and Lily I'd mention how one man had a mustache, the likes of which was seen only in comic opera. A few matching wives, without mustaches, were in attendance, they in fur hats, long coats, and tall boots. Their profiles were of the capital letter D, flat backs and rounded fronts. All seemed to be having a good time. Our bus was off.

I was surprised that the tour guide spoke excellent English, sprinkled with American expressions including, 'very cool' for the lights on the canals' bridges that go up, and stay up for a couple of hours at night to accommodate the commercial water traffic, and 'not cool' for the niche of many lined up caskets of the slaughtered Nicholas and Alexandra family.

"My, my, my." Walking through the church of the heirs of the Romanovs, I bowed my head at their memory.

I was eager to show off my new knowledge. I'd tell the Pennsylvanians, in a pedantic manner, that because of her many, smooth sided concrete canals, Saint Petersburg was named, The Venice of the North. I'd describe the wide and clean rivers without water traffic, at least at this time of the year. No plastic cups or plastic bags floated on the water. There was not a single truck tire, nor an upended grocery cart diverting the stream of water around it. No beggars. I guessed they were somewhere, but not in evidence in the tourist area.

In my next call home I'd mention that we buzzed past the Mariinsky Theater. Nothing going on there tonight.

I wished Kimmy and Lily were here to share Saint Petersburg. I'd send home a book of the city for their perusal and enjoyment, and maybe envy and annoyance that they'd missed the trip. Several excellent book choices were available at the book store. I chastised myself, crazy to be alone on this wonderful journey.

I sighed, straightened and returned my head to the scene. Walking around town, I'd noted the natives walked in two's, including the men, although they didn't hook elbows as the women had. I later observed in my journal, the denizens of the city were well dressed. Boot shops were everywhere. This must be in the city's boot district. I knew New York had various districts for shopping; the diamond district, an avenue of antiques, a street of guitars. I mused, if I were going home to show off the tourist wares, I'd buy official, knee high Russian boots. I brightened, realizing I'd enjoy wearing new Russian leg wear for a few days. I'd send them home before going on to the heat of India, concluding that Kimmy would cheerfully receive her mom's new Russian boots.

There was some competition among the gift shops to attract the tour buses. The driver received a bottle of vodka for delivering a bus filled with tourists to the shop's front door. I had to laugh. I mused as I waited to pay for the easy-to-mail-home nesting dolls and assorted gifts. If Jerry were alive, I'd suggest he employ the bottle of vodka bribery trick with his customers. I splurged on a wooden music box, fashioned after an ornately decorated Saint Petersburg, Russian, onion topped church, a perfect Show and Tell gift for Sara to take to school. Many of the churches were in the process of being gilded. Scaffolding held artisans at work.

On the bus ride back to the hotel I stopped enjoying the tour when the guide swung his arm to the window and reported, "The gray building to your right is the headquarters of the KGB where it is rumored, from the roof, one can see Siberia without binoculars." He had a smirk on his face. There was a twittering of muffled laughter.

I was jolted. How could anyone think that funny? I was spooked. I mumbled, "I need a hot dog and a Coke, and maybe a baseball game and a tranquilizer." I was feeling a long way from home and feeling scared. My brain pronounced, "...not exactly scared, maybe...okay, I'm scared."

To add to my distress, I noticed the same spy hatted man, in the back of the bus. This was the same man whom I'd seen on the first day, the man who seemed to be watching me. When had he gotten on the bus? I wondered if he'd laughed at the 'KGB' remark. Maybe he didn't understand English. I felt nervous and fiddled with my fingers deciding of course he's a spy and he was looking at me again. I gave him a hard look, my chin jutted out. I rearranged my posture, turning to my window, sometimes catching his reflection in the distorted glass.

I felt reassured when a McDonald's hamburger store came into view. Knowing Kimmy and Sara would be entertained to see the long line outside the hamburger palace, I snapped several photos. Thinking about my daughter and granddaughter, a new pang of loneliness stabbed.

Off the bus and back to the hotel, I hurried to my room. After a safe repast of rye crackers and cheese, chased with a handful of spirit building M&Ms, I decided to return to the street of boots to purchase a pair, despite the short remainder of my time in Saint Petersburg. Tomorrow I'd scheduled the Hermitage museum, the next day, a bus ride to Peterhof for a glimpse of the Baltic Sea and the most grandiose palace. "Gold everywhere," I'd heard. One more Wednesday night call to Kimmy and Lily and I'd be off to India.

I wrote: *If I were staying longer, I'd have to go to the American Embassy and look for Yanks. Art makes me want to talk about what I'm seeing. Also, these new black, shiny, Russian boots, with a tiny silver buckle hanging on the strap at the ankle, was a wonderful idea at the time, but are now burning my feet from the inside. Well, that's the problem with not understanding the language. Maybe the smiling saleslady was telling me, "... and if you choose to wear these superior boots indoors, you will die a thousand, screaming deaths of the little known 'Russian Hot Foot' torture."*

I had to agree.

CHAPTER 13

HERMITAGE and COUSINS

After trailing a group of tourists through the Rembrandts at the Hermitage, I surrendered to a marble bench to rest and to peruse my program. I learned Rembrandt's wife was named Saskia. I thought Saskia an interesting name. I'm guessing a derivative of Alexandra. My internal conversation was already considering, too bad the name Saskia didn't make it to America along with the Natalies, Irenas and Valeries. Why was that? Who knew, and who could concentrate?

My feet were roasting. I pulled off my new, butter soft, limp boot from my crying foot. While rubbing my toes, my head snapped up in response to the American words, "Allen, don't go fah, I'll be sitting right he-yah."

I encountered a red-haired woman dressed in an olive green, canvas jacket, identical to mine, my trophy from Fairbanks for being shot. The woman backed up to the bench as she waved off her husband. "You go ahead." She pulled her MIT backpack to her lap, flopped onto the bench within inches of me and digging in the depths, she pulled up a compact package of tissues. She blew her nose, then keeping her head down, cut her eyes to me. I was already smiling at her.

Without a spy's secret handshake or a coded haiku, I said, "Well, hello. Mrs. America. I'm sure glad to see a genuine Unites States woman here in the Hermitage. And look we have matching coats." The woman's mouth dropped open, taking in the English greeting. I hoped I hadn't scared her away, but was eager to speak American to anyone who would understand and perhaps return the conversation.

"Hiii," the redhead drew out, "How ah you?" The woman was a Bostonian who was traveling with her husband on their annual cousins' club vacation. About ten minutes into our laughter with knee slapping, and some snacking on M&Ms, we were joined by the cousins. Introductions all around. As the ladies exchanged information, I became aware I couldn't fit in with this group, even for a day. I kept the secret I was in Russia on a personal quest before going on a balloon trip next week in India, then to die on the fifth of February. The cousins parted with perhaps we'd all see each other later that night at the Swan Lake performance in the Hermitage's famous little theater. We did. We waved across the jewel box auditorium of other patrons on tufted, velvet seats. Maybe they wondered if I were the spy.

I would later document in my journal that watching Russian ballet in Russia was worth the trip. The male dancers were wonderful, thank heaven. Despite the art and talent all around me, my mind wandered. Although the ballet was beautiful, realistically, how many girls grow up to be lifted up by the man? Figuratively, of course. It's the little woman who does all the heavy lifting in a marriage, in mine anyway. This ballet was another hopeful dream for women.

Jerry, it turns out, was a long, yearned for dream, but he seemed to have no true interest in me. I can picture him with his arms lovingly wrapped around me, like the dancers on the stage. Please! Men! But, Stan seems to love Lily. At least he's nice to her, and Kimmy admitted to loving Kevin more than she loved bacon. What an endorsement.

The orchestra was fine. But, sorry to admit, my favorite part of the whole wonderful performance was in the intermission when aiming for a restroom, I climbed narrow, curving stairs. Instead of finding the restrooms, I found comedy in that I opened the door to the dancers' break room. They all snapped to attention from their relaxing, and from doing the unforgiven: smoking cigarettes. Ooops. Dancers smoking! "So sorry." Glad I could play the Russian non-speaking card, I bowed, muttered my foreign tongued apology and backed out.

After the performance, walking back to the hotel room, my boots kicked through two inches of snow. Memories of books and movies about Russia crammed in on me. Becoming teary, I pondered the country's high suicide rate. I felt like crying. I missed my family, American food, the cat, my bed, the kitchen table next to the window looking out to the sloping back yard, Kimmy's kitchen, and Lily's kitchen. Well. I couldn't blame Russia for that. And the good news was the spy wasn't in evidence. "I hope to high heaven I'm not being followed. If I am, I'll bet he doesn't appreciate having to track me in the snow." I chuckled and sang to myself.

Back in my hotel room with Chopin's pianistic gusto on the tape recorder, I chided, and reminded myself my isolation was self-imposed. Because this trip was my thoughtful, well considered choice, I was embarrassed and surprised at feeling blue. Lily would spout how she predicted my remorse. Then she'd further remind me that I was crazy, as was this trip. Guilty as charged, I inhaled a deep cleansing breath and decided to organize for tomorrow's departure. My backpack sagged minus the winter clothes I'd laid out to donate to the church across from the hotel.

I settled in for my nine o'clock call to Pennsylvania. Nine o'clock their time, wee hours in the morning in Saint Petersburg. Yikes. Sleep late tomorrow. My report to Lily and Kimmy covered many subjects. My commentary was a buffet. "They have trolleys with tracks and overhead wires like old Norristown, PA. I feel like I'm in a Russian novel. Never did get a fur hat. I'm loving old Leningrad. Wish you were here." I yammered on about the hot boots I'd be sending home, the Hermitage Museum, the little theater with the ballet dancers who smoked, the church with the ill-fated royal family, the Boston cousins' club. I answered questions about caviar, the expected availability of vodka, the dark sky, the young army men standing about in brown uniforms.

"...and, Kimmy, you should see the beautiful subways. The trains are long, long, long. I'll bet there were fifteen or more subway cars attached to one another, from one end of the station to the other. Looking around you'd swear you were in Philadelphia, except the subway cars and stations are spotless. People all look sober and normal. Some of the advertisements on the wall are in English. No vagrants. No smell of urine!"

Kimmy answered, "So the subways are spotless, but don't drink the water, huh?"

I had to laugh. "Yeah, they can use the tainted water for scrubbing, though. Good thinking, huh? The problem is the antiquated water pipes." The conversation went on to Sara's excellent report card, and Kevin's new car. I suffered more homesickness again. We ended with the usual 'I love you's, and the 'take care's, and it was over until next Wednesday's call from India.

I didn't mention Solzhenitsyn's Black Marias, or the view of a flat piazza that reminded me of a nonspecific black and white photo of heaps of bodies after a mass shooting. Was my memory accurate? Was I giving undue credit to the romantic sadness and isolation I was experiencing? How Tolstoyan. I parried to the angel on my shoulder, "Let's face it, the U.S. is a baby country with no shortage of bloody battles. And, God knows, the bison suffered."

CHAPTER 14

LEAVING RUSSIA and the SPY

Following my day at Peterhof, after a late breakfast in the *Pectopah*, I was becoming eager to leave Russia. I was aware I was dashing into death's arms but felt tired enough to succumb. Interesting, the stitches in my arm were ready to come out right on time to die. I shrugged at the inevitability of the day. I dashed from the hotel to mail the gifts, the boots, and the last batch of photos to Pennsylvania. I caressed my journal knowing I had another week's worth of observations before sending the journal home.

My earlier feelings of sadness were replaced by the happy anticipation of my trip to India. I stood back in my favorite thinking posture, with my arms folded across my chest, and tapped my foot. I reviewed the organized heap of folded clothing on the bedspread; the pile with my passport, airline tickets, the last of my rubles, and the pile of winter clothes waiting to be donated to the church across the street.

The time was right. I still had a few hours before I'd leave the hotel for the airport. I stuck my arms into a lightweight, pale green sweater, the only summer weight item I'd saved for the last air conditioned plane ride. I considered whether or not I'd need my purse. No money would be needed at the church, but at the last minute decided I didn't want it to be stolen from my room, so swung the thing over my arm.

I left the hotel, arms hugging the used winter clothing close to my chest, protecting me against the sudden appearance of the wet, sideways snow. I dashed across the trolley tracks and crossed to the church.

The sign on the outside door advertised the Russian Orthodox church was open all day, every day. A*ch, Mother Russia lives,* I smiled. Up the stone stairs, and into the lighted narthex, I was recognized as a non-Russian and was led toward a stone bench, by a rotund, gray haired woman, without a coat, marking her as an employee. The church woman wore a faded floral print apron worn over a well-used, shin length skirt. She muttered in Russian, swinging her dimpled white arm for me to be seated, then waddled away, to find a priest. I brushed away the slight accumulation of snow from my shoulders and waited.

A solitary umbrella, leaning on the stone bench's edge, clattered to the floor, startling my heartbeat to a temporary rush. My face reddened. The church quieted for a second, then resumed its low private mumblings. I repositioned the culprit umbrella between the wall and the bench, and demurely lowered myself to the cold, flat stone. I sat in my best, straight-backed, prim posture, with my hand on my chest to steady my heart as I waited to be summoned.

The chubby woman returned to her chore of scraping remnants of yellowed bees wax from the glass votive cups, then plopped new votive candles into the wrought iron bank of flickering hopes and prayers. She was the oldest person

I'd seen in Saint Petersburg. I'd be sure to note in my journal that she appeared to be no more than early to mid-fifties.

I tried to affect an expression of disinterest as I waited for the priest. I counted about twenty midday worshippers scattered about the under lit interior, the chapels without church pews. The worshipers posed in prayer at altars and at various religious paintings, preserved under glass. The faithful said their prayer, kissed the glass covering the painting, then shined away the lip smear with a thin cloth for that purpose, hanging on a small rack next to the painting. Nice and neat.

I watched a priest at one side altar worshipping with two well- dressed congregants, maybe girlfriends or co-workers who'd probably ducked into church on their lunch hour. Their heads were covered in scarves, shoulder touching shoulder, their feet tight together making narrow bases as they bent at their waists, bowing in response to the priest's sweeping alb and his sotto voce. I smiled at the image, then inhaled, recognizing the fragrance of the candle wax. Bees wax.

The candles lit up the various altars around the church, as there was no overhead light. Some pale light struggled in through the windows that appeared to be covered by generations of smoke and grime. I decided the church's atmosphere came from candle smoked, dirty, stained glass. I whispered, "Dirty windows. So much for the romantic lighting."

Father Russian Orthodox found me seated with a large heap of clothing on my lap. He introduced his unpronounceable name. I followed him through the candlelit interior. The poor man was hampered with a slow rolling limp. He indicated for me to be seated inside a room with a table and bench and many wooden closets. One open closet door showed the vestments for the services. The priest, with short, clean nails, reached his smooth hands for my donation. He paged through the items with a pleased demeanor, and laid them on a wide table. His anemic smile stretched across crooked teeth. "Da, da. Much tank you, da." He stood to indicate the end of the audience and performed a Russian, backwards sign of the cross in front of my face.

Without a word, the priest indicated the door and escorted me to the narthex. He bowed, turned and limped away. I gave a shallow curtsy, buried my chin in my thin sweater and looked away. I whispered, "Poor guy."

I looked at my watch, calculating that my time to the hotel check out, then heading to the airport, was beginning to close in on me. With my hand pushing on the heavy wooden doors, I turned for a last look around the immense interior, speckled with reflecting gold glinting off the decorations and the glass covered paintings. I stopped abruptly, as if suffering a body blow. I took two steps backwards, startled by the effect of the men's choir starting their warm up in the choir loft overhead. "Oh, thank you. I didn't realize it before, but this is why I came to Russia." With my hotel departure less than two hours off, I settled back against a wall, not realizing my hand had come to rest on my heart.

The men's harmonies were ponderous, very serious, and very Russian. I sat again on the stone bench, placed my purse on the floor behind my crossed feet, the correct posture for a lady in a skirt.

I was touched by the depth and sorrow of the song. The qualities of the despondent, grieving masculine voices brought my twenty-five years of marriage and plus two of widowhood bobbing to the surface. Not a Catholic, I wished for the opportunity for a confession with a priest. I yearned to ask, why was I such a complacent wife? Why the conclusion that if we didn't fight we must be happy? I wasn't happy. I was married, legally tied to a man. I did for him what was expected of me. He had a clean house, clean child, clever conversation, good sex on demand. He had it all. Hell, oh, pardon me, God. I dieted all my adult life for nary the upraised eyebrow of approval. Even our string of pets, over the years, were well behaved.

The men's voices melted together in a thick, velvet ribbon of sound. On a roll of introspection I continued, in thoughts and quiet mumblings, "I was a good tolerant wife, me, not whining and harping about him backing out of ballroom dancing lessons after the first lesson, and we couldn't get our money back."

The angel on my shoulder butted in, "You're whining now. Get over it."

Other angel, other shoulder, "You never got a new car, but instead, got his hand-me-down vehicle. Why was that?"

I didn't know. I was a pretty decent looking, hard-working, faithful, good woman."

Tears rolled straight to my neck scarf, wetting it. I found a tissue in my purse and gave over to quiet, shoulder heaving boo-hooing. The sonorous voices kept singing. "And why did he get so drunk at Kimmy's wedding? Didn't he know his behavior reflected on me? On us?"

105

My tears were renewed. In the loft overhead, the direc-
tor of the men's choir interrupted, in patient, instructive
basso lectures to the group; with rolled 'r's, 'ch's and 'zk'
sounds. I smiled at the remembrance of Robbie's rolled 'r's.
The voices repeated a few bars of the music. They rehearsed
and interrupted several times. A more up-beat piece was
started. This also came with many interruptions. I sniffed,
wiped at my damp nose. I mumbled. "Not to worry, Bevy.
Death comes in a few days and I'm looking forward to it."
I blew my nose into an unfolded tissue, and continued my
reprimand, "Well, old girl, time to go to the hotel and get on
with the show."

I stood and waved good-bye to the woman who had
seated me and gotten the priest for me. I laid ten, filled
to the brim, pastel bags of candy on the stone bench and
signaled to her to take them. No words were exchanged.
She smiled and nodded and made a bee line to the candy
as I hugged my thin sweater around my arms and pushed
through the heavy double doors.

Outside, there was no new snow, but the sky still threatened. Commuters hurried from trolleys and buses to the
corner subway entrance. I concluded if I did not die on
schedule, I'd like to return to Saint Petersburg another time
with a Russian Orthodox Catholic who spoke the language.

I stood on the curb, waiting for traffic and the trolley to
pass. As soon as I stepped into the street, I felt a vigorous
tug on my hand and arm. My purse was ripped from my
grip.

I turned to see the spy hat man running away from
me. He didn't have much speed, but proved he could out

maneuver me. I gritted my teeth, "That dirty dog has been watching me for the entire time I've been here. I guess he has the tourist's schedule figured out, or works with information from the hotel."

He shoved my purse into his coat and ran, turning into a shadowed courtyard between buildings. I followed. The area was filled with randomly parked cars and innumerable exits to the buildings surrounding the court. The buildings appeared to be apartments. People were moving about behind drawn shades. Aromas of food preparation were too innocent for the crime that had just occurred. Voices of families about their business trailed down from some open windows. I stopped chasing, deciding I would not pursue the thief into this well protected hideaway. He'd come after my purse, and he'd gotten it. Tomorrow he'd have a few useless keys, and a few kopecks and I'd be in India. And thank GOD, Russia's God, my passport and travel tickets were still on my bed in the hotel.

My last note to Lily from Russia:

Tomorrow is the last of January. I'm off to India. Have mailed the boots for you or Kim; whoever fits in them. Ahhh, I can see you two sitting like Cinderella's sisters taking turns, trying on my boots. For the record, the Russian words for Gesundheit, after a sneeze, in Russian, sounds like, "Boots 're off!" When you take off your boots, I'll be saying, 'God bless you.' So that's that. In an hour I'll be brave and dash through the frosty evening chill to the cab to the airport, then on to India and into hot sunshine.

This trip is going well, still enjoying seeing the world of difference from Pine Bluffs. Two stops and so far two men putting moves on me, both nice looking, and a third, not so nice, stole my purse.

CHAPTER 15

DEADLINE in INDIA

After writing a few words under the title of *My Very Last Day 2-5-98*, I looked up to the leaves of the tree, changed the position of my legs, tapped the pen against my pursed lips wondering where to begin? I leaned to the tablet and wrote a few words mentioning the hotel's narrow bed, and recounted the black birds' early morning ruckus outside my window.

The sounds and fragrance of the morning were distracting. I listened to the language of the morning; no English, but the high pitched voices of boys running to school, the jingle of the biker's bells, the nasal "rrrmmm" of the few motorized scooters. Pedicabs drove by the hotel, while foot traffic was picking up. Unable to concentrate, and without the philosophic wisdom to summarize my feelings about my "last day," I slid my pen and notebook into my backpack.

I shooed the buzzing flies from my sticky slice of pounded apricot. I swallowed the last of the tea, dusted the almond biscuit crumbs from my lips. The music, "*The Mighty Quinn*," became faint, then nonexistent as a woman slid into the Land Rover driver's seat, and drove the teens away from the square. I closed my eyes to review my plans for the day. My heart fluttered. I asked myself, "Getting stage fright as the hour closes in?" My answer, "Yes."

I'd paid ahead for the full balloon trip from the outskirts of old Madras. Float up, travel for a few miles, then down again. The colorful trifold advertisement from the travel agent showed the balloon ride to take the gondola with five or six passengers for a distance of about ten miles. After the trip, the balloon would touch down in a field where we would be met by a truck or car, horses, or a cart. It was not much of a distance to float, but promised to be a mind blowing experience, plus it got me, at last, to Madras, renamed Chennai.

If the short sequence of numbers was predicting my death, as I was sure they were, well, I'd face it. I'm a genius for conceiving this trip, I concluded again. Lily will be disappointed I never kissed a snake's head. She's right though, because, in Pine Bluffs, anything more dangerous than keeping the house clean is taking a risk. "Hell, I never did anything other than dishes and dust. After Kimmy moved out, I kept things going in the house, doing more for the church, meetings, baking and, well, everything." I sighed. Tears were back.

What a pitiful little life I'd had. I'm not much different from those Indian women I read about, who lived their whole lives in their father's, then their husband's homes and courtyards. "But that was then," I said aloud.

I felt a slight tug at my backside. I swiped my hand across my buttocks without looking back and knocked my hand into something wet. "Yikes." I jumped and looked around to see a white Brahmin bull nuzzling at the back of my jacket. "Holy cow!" The bull nodded and blinked, like an official introduction had happened. I jumped to my feet spilling my shoulder bag to the ground. A few boys pointed and laughed as the bull, rebuffed by my aggressive scream and waving hands, he huffed a breath and plodded away.

My heart was flipping around at the startle. I grabbed my shoulder bag, then backed to lean against the tree trunk, protecting myself from another rear assault. I caught my breath then, looking at the trifold advertisement one more time, I reviewed: The bus I awaited would drop me off at the crossroads depot on the other side of the Rose River in about two hours or so. Then, if all worked according to schedule, I would be met by someone from *Das Bruder Brucke Ballons* and would be driven to Madras, where other extreme vacationers would join the party for a balloon ride.

Squinting in the direction of the expected bus, I checked my watch again. My rapid heartbeat reminded me that the bull had given me quite the scare, the sort I'd never have experienced in Pennsylvania. I'd be watching a junior league basketball game, as I had done every year in my memory.

I leaned back against the tree and peered into the small leaves of the branches overhead. "I can't believe I'm here in India. Too bad I had to become a widow to pull off this trip. But Jerry would never have come out of Pennsylvania. He would never take more than five days leave from his laundry company. What was his problem?"

My attention was drawn to a group of women, all in traditional saris, kicking the colorful hems of their skirts as they scurried past the hotel I'd just left. I noticed how these women were like the Russian women in whose personal space in their cluster was closer than the Americans tolerate. I smiled recalling how the Russian women walked in step, elbows linked, shoulder to shoulder.

My argument about Jerry resurfaced in my personal debate. How hard could it be to run a laundry that catered to two hospitals, four nursing homes and a hospice? Collect the sheets and towels. Honest to God, it's not as if he had to decorate the darned sheets or do anything complicated, a glorified diaper service, collect, wash, dry and fold 'em and return the dumb things. What did that take?

"God, I'm such a peacemaker. I always put up with his lukewarm to non interest in anything I had to say. He always said he was 'sooo busy.' He had a puny three trucks, three drivers, three paychecks, and then the washing machines. How many machines were there? Thirty, forty of them, give or take. How often did I hear about a machine or a dryer breaking? Never. I'm guessing the foreman did all the repairs. He got it taken care of, because how complicated is it to fix or replace a washer? Not as if he had to send to Japan or Germany for parts, for heaven's sake. How many people worked in the laundry? Nine. He had seven machine operators, and Sam, foreman and day supervisor, and Ernie, the evening man. Add the custodian, the two office bees, Peggy and Doris, our trusty two old Girls of Summer, and the drivers. So that's,…" I looked down and counted on my fingers, three, nine, looked into the blue, " Uhhh, fifteen, seventeen employees. Hell, Jerry could have gotten away for a vacation. Everyone else did. Sam could have covered for him." I snapped my head straight up from my counting, "Shit! It all sounds too easy. Maybe the business was a front for the REAL activity! Maybe *he* was a spy.

A money launderer? A two-timing bastard? Yeah, that's it. Two-timing. He wasn't smart enough for real crime."

I sat up straight and snapped my fingers. "Maybe, he didn't want to get away." A girlfriend! At work? Peggy? She was the younger of the two, and cute enough. Maybe there'd been some chicky somewhere out of town. Away from me! That would explain why Doris and Peggy shut up so fast that time I brought the bedspread into the shop when I'd knocked the red wine all over the bed. Boy, they were overly solicitous toward me.

"But I'm in India today on the trip of my life. Leave it alone." I flopped backwards against the tree. Speechless, thoughtless, I looked at my watch. "Where's the darned bus? I'll be late for the balloon ride. One doesn't want to screw up one's death date."

I snapped a look to my left, then my right. I hope I hadn't been moving my mouth and swinging my fist around. If someone saw me sitting here arguing with myself they might have me arrested, in India. Aye-yi-yi. "Boy, that would be an interesting postcard, from the local hoose-gow!" I laughed aloud, stood and circled the tree, looking at the pink-white pebbles on dusty ground. I tapped my hand on my thigh, impatient with the late bus and with my past history of acquiescence. I looked to the sky.

I was so darned mad I wanted to live past the date of 2-5-98, so I could go home again to question those two good old birds in the office. Maybe the whole town knew. "Hey, I wonder if Kimmy and Lily knew about Jerry's infidelity, IF he'd been cheating. Aw, shucks, if everyone in town knew, I would have known too, right?" The jury in my head quieted.

"Having a double life could have been what killed him. God, I'll have to think about this later.

A noisy engine lifted my attention to see my scheduled conveyance of a rickety bus, bounce into view. The bus was Ticonderoga #2 pencil, yellow, and reminded me of a Walt Disney cartoon creation. A few windows were missing, but as the "Mañana" song observed, one didn't need a window on "such a sunny day." The cloud of dust that followed the bus at a safe distance, caught up with, and overtook the vehicle when it rumbled to a stop in front of the hotel. At eight in the morning about a dozen passengers were already on the bus, two women half hung out of the opened and absent windows to have a look at the hotel and the next passenger.

A rotund, smiling, and sweaty bus driver nodded to me, opened his left hand in a grand swooping gesture inviting me into the bus. I was the only passenger to board from the square in front of the hotel. I pushed my sunglasses onto my forehead, hoisted my backpack and shoulder bag and climbed aboard. My view of the other passengers was a quick glance, not to make them uncomfortable with my perusal of them. How long had they been riding? It was so early to already be aboard a bus, traveling the countryside.

I took a bench seat for three, backing up to the window. I sat after pushing my pretty purple luggage into a rack over my head, thinking with a moment of pride of how organized and together my luggage looked. Me, world traveler. The rack seemed to have been welded overhead when the bus was converted to passenger transport from an old school bus. Then, why hadn't they repainted this one to look like all those other beautiful, brightly painted buses? Maybe it's a work in progress, like the rest of us. Oh, well, not my worry.

I was mindful as a foreigner to not visually confront the others, but rather to let them have a good long look at me. Sitting across the aisle and facing me was a sixtyish man wearing a full-headed toupee as stiff and black as patent leather. He wore dark rimmed glasses. He was holding, what appeared, by familiarity and resemblance, to be his grandson, maybe four-years-old, whom he called Asi. The child's eyes were shaped like two perfect, smooth mint leaves. His cheeks still had the softness and pink flush of babyhood. The two whispered to one another as the grandfather nuzzled the cheek of the beautiful child. Both had the same caramel colored skin and each was dressed rather formally for such a hot morning. The grandfather had a bundle on the seat next to him, and an open white paper sack, that seemed to hold edibles. At intervals, the man dipped his hand into and out of the bag, dropping a morsel into his mouth. The two were enjoying tangling their fingers and poking each other, the sort of entertainment I'd found tiresome with my own grandchild.

The older man caught me watching his cherished grandson, and in one English word stated, "Buthday" indicating the boy with the tilt of his head, and direction of his eyes. He whispered to the smiling little boy who held up four fingers for me to count. I smiled at the child who was born on February fifth. How coincidental. God bless this patient old gentleman and his treasure.

I found myself smiling at the boy. His dimpled knees reminded me of Sara's many dimples. So sweet. So sweet. I unzipped my belly pack and withdrew my keychain, embellished with a small, silvery, dangling moose, that I'd purchased in Fairbanks. I plucked the trinket from the keys. My raised eyebrows asked permission from the grandfather. I dangled the little moose in front of the child, saying, "Happy Birthday." The boy smiled up at me, then snapped up the shiny moose. The grandfather attached the keychain through a belt loop on the child's shorts. The boy sat back, smiled and fingered his unexpected birthday gift.

I decided to guild the lily on this occasion, and dug around in my back pack for another little gift. I produced a yellow gauze bag of the sturdy chocolates, still not melted in India's heat. The old man smiled, turning his attention to the boy, and offered the child a chocolate M&M. He ate one, himself. Both were happy with their birthday celebration.

I, too, smiled and sat back with a surreptitious glance at the rest of the passengers. I noted a solitary masculine passenger sitting in the middle of the bus. He looked like a proper Englishman. Presumably he was a businessman by the way he was intent on his scribbling and ignoring everything around him. He wore a thin mustache, and topped off his head with a straw hat. His mouth was an absolute straight line, a dash. He made notations in a red notebook as he withdrew papers, scribbled on them one at a time, reread and returned them to the briefcase. He was preoccupied with his figuring, and never showed any interest,

116

or even awareness of the bus and its inhabitants. This ride must be old stuff to him.

A group of middle-aged women, all of whom seemed to know one another, took up the seats in the back of the bus. They sat close to each other talking, laughing, and pointing at the scenery, which for my money was pretty uninteresting. The chattering women were in filmy pastel saris, with ribbon and small jewels twisted into center parted, braided, long dark hair. Bundles wrapped in paper, fastened with hemp, were piled on the seats and the floor next to the women. Their main identifying characteristic was how much fun they seemed to be having, laughing and talking behind their hands. They created a pastel, colorful bouquet, not choosing to spread out to the many seats available to them.

We bucked along on pretty good springs for such a funny old bus. The bus kept the cyclone of dust and dirt trailing behind, like the shoes and cans tied to the bumper of a car marked, "Just Married."

The scenery was stony, dry and gently sloping downward toward the river. The ground was flat and uninteresting, but come to think of it, if I'm going to board a balloon, I'd want a flat geography, no forests or mountains. On second thought, boring is a pretty good idea. Giving credit where it was due, the sky was a clear turquoise, un-dotted by clouds.

I had not taken a photo since snapping a picture of the samovar back at the hotel. After two hours of smiling and nodding, I realized I was no longer under scrutiny of the women, and could take a few impromptu, casual shots of the passengers and the interior of the bus. God was in heaven, and all was well with the world, I concluded. A few photos later, and the camera went back into the belly pack. Birds boldly fluttered near the bus. The river and the boxy white depot on the other side were dead ahead. Next, last, a balloon ride.

The Rose River appeared to be about two football fields wide. The languid water's flow created a picturesque scene. Designed for function without any pretense of beauty, the bridge was supported by steel support beams, with the roadway sided by short concrete walls.

A few flat barges were lined up close to the river banks. A single sizable barge floated near the bridge in the middle of the river. Upstream, adults fished from the sloping bank. Children and a few dogs tumbled and splashed around in the shallow water. Squat, square stucco walled structures on both sides of the river were picturesque and worthy of a photo. I could not decide if the structures were homes or businesses. Several men and two donkeys lolled in the shade of the building nearest the bridge. Many cars, motorcycles and bicycles, some old, some new, were parked in a random pattern near the buildings. I wanted to document the scene. I whispered to no one, "Well, it isn't the L.A. freeway, but it's a busy intersection of highway, river, barges, man, beast and child. Worth a few photos."

As the bus started across the bridge I unzipped the camera from my belly pack, rhythmically tapping a foot and softly singing the words, *"Come on without, come on within, You'll not see nothing like the Mighty Quinn, Come on within, ..."* I brought the camera to my eye to center the kids on the bank when I was thrown from my balance. The bus swerved a sharp left. The drunken jolt was followed by the bus jerking to the right and into the empty oncoming traffic lane. The salesman's open case hit the floor with a flat crack, adding to the startle effect, while the ladies' many bundles flew into lateral and vertical motion. The passengers hollered in one pitch and loudness. We all scrambled to regain our seats and footing and grabbed for hand holds as the bus lurched again to the left, crashing into the short concrete side wall of four-foot square supports holding flat cross beams of concrete.

The impact caused us to tumble into one another again, crashing painfully into the seat backs and to the floor. Arms and legs and soft silky midriffs hit against the bus's walls and into metal frames of the seats, and into one another. Heads and limbs were bruised and bleeding, unable to stop their own destruction. Packages hit against panicky faces and bounced to the down slanting ceiling.

CHAPTER 16

ROSE RIVER ACCIDENT

The next is the memory of the accident I hope will fade away as bad dreams dissipate like smoke. The tragedies I saw happened in an instant, as I tumbled, grabbed a seat back and held on, hit the floor and pulled myself between two front facing seats. I watched the bridge wall give out in a puff of white concrete, powdering at the impact, showering small pebbles, shooting a cloud of white dust into the air. I heard the frantic, high pitch of the passengers' voices contrasted in octaves to the groan and squeal of the twisting bridge supports as the steel folded on itself. I watched the horizon betray us, tilting to become diagonal, as our bus headed into the river. The driver tumbled from his seat, with his knees pulled up to his chest. He rolled like a ball into the stairwell where his backside wedged on the lowest step. A leg sticking straight up from the stairwell prevented him from pulling himself from his crumbled position.

The old man with his grandson on his lap slid from his seat, thudding against the front window. His head smacked back, crashing against the front, rear view mirror. His glasses flew from his face as he reflexively, conscientiously, cradled Asi's little body and head to his chest. Asi's face hit into his grandfather's chin, then bounced down to catch his lip on the old man's tie tack. Asi screamed at the sight of his grandfather's blood and at the dislodged toupee covering his grandfather's left eye. The bus's impact caused the old man's ghoulish, sneering, false teeth to be pushed forward, now two inches from Asi's face. My heart wanted to comfort the child but my hands needed to hold on to the seat back.

The unfortunate bus was airborne and heading left toward the Rose River. The impact of the bus on the water caused us to bounce from our first landing places. Voices squealed in disbelief and panic. The nose of the bus settled into the river bottom's loose silt, the front three windows taking on water. The remaining back windows and door bobbed above the broiling water.

White lacy tips of river water pulled billows of clear brown water behind, into the bus's open windows. The businessman imitated Santa Claus in Clement Moore's poem, "… *he said not a word but went straight to his work* …" Was it panic that kept me frozen in place? I was the observer, unable to move. I watched the salesman step from his shoes, pull his hat onto his head, and without his briefcase, hurried up the aisle, above the waterline to the rear of the bus. His weight caused the bus to dip. The women clustered near the rear, screamed and reached for one another. He pushed himself through an absent rear window frame, splashed into the water, and was gone.

The river continued to spill through the open windows in the front of the bus. The unforgiving Rose River closed over the puffed cheeked, red faced bus driver's head. The grandfather squeezed his eyes shut to the driver's hand wagging back and forth. He cooed to his grandson trying to cover the boy's screams as he struggled to his feet, petting the child's head. The bus sank no farther.

The ladies huddled together crying and calling in loud, high hysterical notes. A frantic, portly woman screamed as she slapped at the folds of her wet sari floating up around her middle tire of a bare midriff. The brown water stain inched up her diaphanous skirt to her waist. She slapped at the erratic movement in her skirt. She redoubled her scream as she pulled a rather large, startled, flopping fish from the tangle and folds of her sari. She beheld the fish in disbelief, holding it as far from her body as possible, continuing her uninterrupted scream. She flung the wriggling fish back into the water, now at the level of her hips, and shook her hand in the air as if to rid herself of the sensation of the fish in her hands.

I watched in a stupor. My nose and forehead were bleeding. A raw scrape ran down the full length of my left shin. My khaki shorts and under pants were torn up to the waistband, hanging open like a skirt. Blood ran down to my sock and trailed off in an oily red thread into the river water. My left shoulder ached and a red lump rose near my elbow. Time slowed to etch the details into my memory of every happening around me.

"Oh, my God, 2598 has come to claim me." I regarded my throbbing, injured arm. My mind raced. So, now it comes. "Oh, God, this is IT. I knew it." But did I really, really think it was possible? I thought my numbers were a cute and clever game I'd been living out. The last music I heard was, "The Mighty Quinn." My last meal was biscuit and apricot. Why are these sweet people in the bus wreck with me? What sense does this make? How can this be? Tears streamed down my face. Did I make this happen to all of these innocent people? I should have leapt into a deep chasm in an Alaskan glacier, alone. What have I done?

I wiped the blood and tears from my face with the back of my hand while surveying the suffering and hurt around me. At least one person got out. I was aroused from my catatonia and inner dialogue by the moaning and wailing of the women, struggling toward the back of the bus, so far, un-flooded. I looked up to see the grandfather pushing his legs through the force of the river water, holding his crying, treasured child close to him. In words I could not understand, but which meaning I could not miss, the old man thrust the boy into my arms. Asi protested with screaming, feet kicking, head wagging and his pummeling hands pushing me away. His fingers desperately dug into his grandfather's collar and neck. His grandfather was doing the unthinkable, surrendering him to a stranger. The patient old man cooed to the child, never taking eyes from me, nodding, assuring me this task must be done. Wasn't he going to save himself? My thoughts were screaming. And what about all the women? Wouldn't they try to get out of the back of the bus?

I grabbed Asi, feeling his dissenting vote with his steady kicking into my thigh and upper leg. I struggled with the child, clamping his hands down to his side to avoid his flailing fists, and like the businessman, I climbed uphill in the center aisle, through the water to the back window. The rear door of the bus was too high above the water for me to drop the child into the river. I'd lose him.

Feeling powerless as I searched for an alternative escape route, I turned toward the middle of the bus where I could ease myself and the screaming boy, together, through the absent window into the water. I walked Asi to the back windows, pushing past the women in the aisle. He resisted with every bit of his strength.

I called, "Stop it, stop it!" struggling to pin his arms down. He answered in screams and battling with his released arms and legs. I renewed my strong grip on him and shoved him out through the same window the businessman had used. I clung to the fighting, twisting little wrist. I followed my own hand through the window, and landed inches from Asi's head in choppy water that quickly covered both of us.

I could see the bright sky lighting the layer of glinting water over our heads. I furiously kicked to propel Asi above me to break his head through the glassy lid of the Rose River. In pushing him ahead of me, Asi kicked out, landing a shoe in my chest. I followed to the surface, coughing water and gasping for breath. The sun lit up the churning waves, blinding me. Asi clung to my head sending us both, again, beneath the river's rough surface. I kicked to the top and repositioned the boy against my body.

The cold water shocked Asi. He pulled his knees to his chest as he breathed without sound. His cheeks sucked in and out and his teeth chattered. His eyes darted from side to side while blood and mucous ran from his nose to his bloody, downturned, bitten lower lip. Thin weeds clung like a scar across his cheek, and reached up and tangled in his black hair.

My ears were filled with water making my voice sound like a stranger's. I called in a new voice, "Asi, Asi," pulling him closer. His fisted hands now ceased to pummel, but held on to me in a strangling grip. I hung onto him and side-stroked for the closest shore, in the direction the bus had been heading. The bus groaned and rocked on the water behind us.

Asi surrendered to my design. His wide, brown, fright-filled eyes watched the water. What had he seen? What would he remember? I continued to swim despite my inability to loosen his grasp, pinching my shirt at my neck. He pulled-in deep sobs and continued to watch, cling and choke me. In one second his life had changed forever.

What a tragedy. My thoughts scrambled. I wanted to pray, but I was out of my country where my God lived. I was in a country of other gods and of other worship. I couldn't speak this god's language. I was sure my God was every-where. That's what we learned: "God is Everywhere," and He would hear my desperate plea for help.

Yet, prayers would not form in my mouth, but I could swim. I looked behind to see the back of the bus had not submerged. The ineffective taillights continued to blink rhythmically above the lapping brown river. The upper body of one of the women poked above the bus's now open back door. She was wild, calling and waving. Two others joined her at the open door, their weight causing a sudden groan of the bus as its rear dipped closer to the river. Thank heaven the women were trying to get out. Screams followed.

126

I pushed on, spitting out dirty river water that had slapped into my mouth. Asi looked at my face when I spoke aloud, but he made no sound. He pointed to a small black dog swimming past. The dog's mouth was open, tongue out, appearing as if he were smiling ear to ear. Was the dog from the shore or from a car on the bridge? An overturned car near the riverbank had all of its four wheels, like the feet of a dead animal, in the air. The rear wheels were still turning, uselessly, spilling rivulets of water from the rotating treads. I couldn't look. My heart was wrung out with pain. Others had died or would die because of this accident. Why were they suffering because of my numbers?

Thank God, my feet touched the silty bottom of the river, the answer to my unasked prayer. Clothed and soaked people walked from the river. Had these people come from the shore or from other cars? Panicky voices called to others on the banks. I stopped in knee deep water and turned back to look at the bus. A glance showed the bridge support had been knocked over by the barge, the same barge that I had earlier observed from the ill-fated bus. I did not see more than a few cars in the river.

I'd gotten out. The others on the bus saw how I did it. They could do it. Surely Asi's grandfather and the women would be saved somehow.

Despite his inability to understand my language, I kept talking to Asi, the unfortunate birthday boy, calling him by name, trying to reassure him with my voice. I was startled when a handsome young man dressed in the same formal style as Asi's grandfather marched toward Asi and me at the water's edge, reached down and ripped the boy from my tight grasp. He said nothing, but was brusque and pushed me aside as if I were trying to abscond with the child. Asi screamed something like "Pah" then swung his hands out to the wild-eyed young woman who followed her husband into the shallow river. The mother making loud ululations, likewise tore the child from her husband's grasp. She swiped water, blood and weeds from her child's face, her voice softening as she pulled him to her body. They abruptly twisted away from me and struggled up the bank where the mother weaved and collapsed to her knees. The husband, in an ancient, symbolic protective posture, stretched his arms around his wife and child. I thought how they resembled the Russian nesting dolls I'd sent home to Sara. Their reunion was a rude miracle. Asi renewed his wail. The three huddled on the ground, rocking and crying. The parents looked past me, to the yellow bus's rear end showing above the river, protruding like an inappropriate lemon wedge in dark tea. The small family sat, dazed and not moving from their place, perhaps waiting for the next miracle; waiting for the grandfather to emerge from the water.

I bent down to pet Asi's head to show my understanding and relief at their reunion, but the parents did not acknowledge me. I noticed the silver moose still attached to Asi's belt loop and knew he'd have quite the story to explain.

CHAPTER 17

NEW DAY

Hugging my injured left arm to my side, I trudged up the riverbank to Das Bruder Brucke Ballon Jeep parked in the shade of a cluster of trees. Arriving at the rear bumper, I bent low, and vomited. I straightened and put my hand to my throbbing head. Again, no prayers would come, other than my words of despair, "O, God, O, God." Perhaps I could go back to the bus for the grandfather. No. Who was I kidding? I couldn't even stand up.

The German driver of the Jeep was wearing a khaki jumpsuit that zipped from his knee to his neck. "Wolfgang" was sewn on his left chest. He carried a radio microphone. "Help is on the way," he reassured in several languages to the scattered knots of witnesses on the bank. Rowboats materialized from the shore as others stood in the shallow water observing from a safe distance. Spectators watched with their fists propped on their hips or held a hand at their foreheads, shielding their eyes from the sunshine.

I was feeling faint and unsure on my feet. I collapsed to a bench in the shade of a spindly tree, then shivering, lifted myself on wobbling legs, to the warmth of the sunlight on the crinkled, brown grass. I propped my head on my arms and started to cry, this time with long moans and gasps.

The commentator in my brain reminded me despite today's date's numbers being 2-5-98, I was still alive. I regarded my cuts and bruises and rubbed away thin tracks of blood with dry grass pulled from the dusty soil. I permitted a weak smile at the knowledge that Asi was alive. From where I sat, I could see the bus's rear, still bobbing above the dark river, and saw little boats rowing toward its back door. I was sure others would be brought to safety.

"I have to call Lily. She won't believe my story. She'll say today's numbers were, instead of my death, the day I saved the life of a young boy. But that was important, wasn't it? If I hadn't been there, no one would have saved him. Oh, I can't even think about that."

"*Fraulein, kann ich dir helfen?...*" I looked up to the urgent speech to see the efficient Wolfgang Brucke, of Das Bruder Brucke fame, no longer using his walkie-talkie, but spending his worried attention on me.

I interrupted, "English?"

"Miss," he said extending a blue woolen blanket he'd pulled from under a seat of the truck.

I thanked the man, not bothering to hide my red eyes and tear streaked face. I was suddenly aware that the rent in my shorts and underwear showed skin and beyond. I was conflicted with being embarrassed and being too weak and used up to do anything about it. Receiving the blanket, I wrapped myself in the sturdy material. I introduced myself as a balloon customer. He looked at the clipboard on the front seat and said, "Oh, yes, Mrs. Bevfferly Schuler.

"Vat an unhappy day for you on a vacation. You have come so far chust to suffer such a tragedy," he said in accented English, and with such heartfelt emotion. "Vere you alone, or perhaps you were traveling viss your husband, or children?"

"Oh, no, I'm alone, but much to my surprise, I'm alive. And, happy that the little kid over there is too." I sniffed and ran my hand under my nose, "But, I don't know how lucky the others from the bus are."

"Ahhh, yes, I saw the child viss his parents. You carried him to safety. You haff done a vonderful sing, a blessed sing," he said, pronouncing each "w" sound as a "v" and the actual "v"s like "f"s. I ran his words through the translation gyrus of my brain as he spoke in a halting English. I understood him about four words after he spoke them.

"Oh, madam, you haff blessed zis family many fold. You vill be granted a long life for your good deed. That handsome youngster is fery special in this province. Almost considered royalty."

Mr. Wolfgang Brucke leaned down to my hunched figure, pulling me up to my full height. With an arm around my shoulders he helped me to his Jeep. I cried aloud with his pressure on my arm. He winced in sympathy and relocated his leading grasp.

"Come, let's get you to a hospital for an over look. A look over."

I interrupted, "Oh, no. I have a few scratches and bruises. Nothing worthy of a hospital visit. I'll be fine. Maybe to a hotel to clean up and rest, if you'll come back to get me for the balloon trip."

He stood back to look at my whole body. He nodded in agreement, satisfied with my self-assessment. "I'm sure you

131

haff many calls to make. Ve vill reschedule the balloon ride to another day if you are still interested. And please call me 'Volf.'"

"Who's saving all the others in the bus? All those beautiful ladies?" I cried my question.

"You can see there are many boats going to the rescue. Don't worry. Others will be saved."

He assisted me to the vehicle's front seat, noting, "There were no other balloon customers today, so I shall take you to Chennai." I wasn't interested in conversation, stared straight ahead, and being exhausted to my sinews, slumped to the shoulder of the generous driver. Wolfgang looked down on me, taking in my river matted hair and bloody forehead. He whispered something, sounding soothing, in German.

I frowned as I translated two words in the phrase I understood. German I and II in high school had earned me an "A," but I'd had no intention of speaking, or translating German ever again after graduation. *Kleine madchen? Little girl?* What is he saying?

I was aroused from sleepiness when the shoeless English businessman, who'd escaped from the back of the bus and appeared to be in top form, ran to the driver's side of the Jeep. He kept up with the moving vehicle for a few paces, barking for help and requesting passage to a specific street in Chennai. Wolf stopped, opened his hand, and gestured toward the empty back seat. The Englishman introduced himself as a representative of Smithy Industries. Wolf nodded and asked no questions and did not engage the Englishman in conversation.

The salesman settled himself in a slump, propping his elbow on a box of Das Bruder Brucke Ballons advertisements on the seat next to the window. Without his briefcase and notations to scribble, he leaned his proper head against his hand, and rolled his eyes beneath closed thin blue lids. His clothes had been drenched, but otherwise he was unscathed. He showed no evidence of injury. No river debris clung to his clothes, nor skin, and somewhere along his post-river tragedy, he managed to comb his hair, including a neat part. I asked myself, "How can he sleep?" Wolfgang started the Jeep and we were off through flat, dusty, scrubby land.

Close to an hour later, we three were in the confines of the city of Chennai. I wanted to enjoy the bustle of the old city, but could not. I knew if I did not get to a hotel soon, I was going to cry, long and loud.

The old putty faced Englishman was delivered to his approved destination. Wolfgang hopped out and like one of Cinderella's footmen, held the rear door open. The man unbuttoned his rear pocket and pulled out damp, folded money, peeled off two bills and thanked Herr Brucke for his help. Wolfgang started to refuse the money, but looked at me, took pity, and accepted the pay. Mr. Englishman gave a polite little bow to the German, turned on his shoeless feet and marched to the hotel's revolving door.

"Stiff upper lip and all that, chip, chip." Wolf said in a feigned British accent returning to the driver's seat.

I was weary. I shook my head and croaked above a whisper, "Giving credit where it's due, I wouldn't have been so clear headed in getting out of the bus if I hadn't watched him." With my thumb pointing over my shoulder, I said, "He was calm. He kicked off his shoes, walked to the back of the bus and pushed himself out through an open window."

Wolf spoke as he kept his eyes on the road. "He was no hero." His accent was becoming more understandable to me. He slowed his English delivery but not giving me a chance to add a word to his discourse. "I, and others on the depot side of the river watched in horror as your bus sailed to the river. Your bus bounced on the water. We did not know if there were survivors. We stood in random groups and covered our mouths to not cry aloud. Some ran back to the depot's phones. Some started into the river in row boats. Others swam. Then, as if a tiny ant crawled over the lip of a jam jar, Mr. Englishman appeared at the back window of the bus. He was alone. In time we could hear the cries of women, but we saw no other person. Then you and the child appeared. I had to run to the truck to use my walkie-talkie radio, you call it.

"Oh," I said aloud when I translated 'cham char' to jam jar. All his 'j's were 'ch's. But his eyes were so warm, and voice so soothing. I was getting sleepy again. I'd trust this Cherman to drive me wherever he wanted to drive.

"When I came back to the river, I could not find you. By that time the river was filled with people going out to the bus and to the other cars that followed your bus into the water. This is indeed a sad day."

Brucke continued, "That man marched up strong through the Rose River as if he were Moses with his people coming through the river. But he had no other people with him as you had. He did not call for help for the others. He thought of himself. He took his hat off … can you imagine, he still had his hat on his head … and slapped it against his leg." Wolf demonstrated swiping his hand across the top of his leg. "Then, he squinted through the bright sunlight at all the activity on the river, and took a comb from his back pocket and smoothed his hair. He was the perfect gentleman standing in a summer suit, observing the chaos and death from a safe distance."

Jumping back in the driver's seat, Wolfgang Brucke spouted a full, cheery German sentence to me, either forgetting my inability to understand, or not wanting me to know what he said. He wheeled into traffic and came to a sudden stop at a store front with a large window. Smiling, he indicated with a wave and an upheld index finger, for me to wait.

Within fifteen minutes, Mr. Brucke, toting a parcel under his arm climbed back into the driver's seat. He placed the package on my lap. He said in his best, accented English, "Hold this. I'll explain later. I am confident the Englishman would want to share his money with you."

I turned the package in my hands and propped my head on my arm on the open window. Wolf started speaking before he was aware my eyes had closed. "Ve must haff a plan."

Feeling drunk, or too tired to hide my smile, I nodded agreement. He's charming, all right.

Whipping the vehicle through traffic, we arrived at a hotel. He continued to be solicitous and gallant and continued to call me, Mrs. Bevfferly Schuler. I noted no numerals on the façade of the hotel. The neighborhood was somewhat

135

of an upgrade from the salesman's hotel. Inside the lobby, holding my uninjured arm, Wolf indicated with his head toward me as he spoke to the desk clerk. I continued to swath myself in the blanket to cover my indecent situation.

I was grateful Wolfgang spoke English. He took several bills from a wallet as he directed, "Please arrange for a doctor to see Mrs. Schuler. She was involved in a tragic bus mishap in the Rose River a few hours ago. A most unlucky day for many of the passengers. No, no luggage. Her property is still in the Rose River."

He took the room key, number 603, and keeping to my slow pace, escorted me to my room. I couldn't complain. I exhaled a secret sigh of relief when I saw the numerals on the key had not a two, a five, not a nine, nor an eight in the sequence. Too weak to smile, I watched the generous man open the hotel door. He busied himself around the rather ordinary hotel room, turning on the light, turning down the bedspread. I yawned and covered a smile. "This room is a whole lot fancier than where I slept last night." I was remembering the single bed with a sagging mattress, and no water glass on the side table.

I fingered the string on the package Mr. Brucke had handed to me, then set the parcel on the bureau. He led me to the edge of the double bed, and as if I were a child, pressed my shoulders for me to sit. He spoke a soothing German. He folded down the sheet and bedspread. He went to the bathroom, turned the sink faucets on, then off, and test-flushed the toilet. He mumbled something in German that sounded to me like a satisfied remark that all was in order.

Still speaking German he saw my eyebrows up in question. He switched to English and repeated his message. "If you feel you need the hospital, I'll take you there now."

I refused medical care a second time. Looking into my face, he reassured that the hotel would send in a doctor, or perhaps they'd take me to the doctor. The man at the desk was not sure if a physician came into the hotel during hospital hours. But, he promised I'd be safe during my stay.

Wolf went on to recommend that I have a hot shower to remove the dirty river water from my body and clothes. He added that this hotel had hot water 'round the clock, and he'd paid at the desk, in the amount of my unused balloon ride. "Zo, you can haff food sent up, make phone calls, and pay for medicine." He ended with the paternal advice, "Get some rest now."

Indicating the parcel I'd placed on the bureau, Wolfgang said, "Mrs. Schuler, because your own clothes are so torn and hurt, you will need these. You haff here a skirt that will fit any lady size, so you have something to cover you up. And a fresh shirt, or blouse, how do you call it?" He changed the subject. "If you're feeling better, no matter what, please, don't go out by yourself."

I unwrapped my blanket to assess my torn shorts and water-stained jersey top. I was acutely aware my left bare leg and hip were exposed up to my waist. I pulled the two edges of the ripped shorts together, although the shredded sides could not be closed. Wolf looked away.

Wolf said, "Some of the money is from that English fellow. He could afford it. Don't worry." Wolf laughed as he plumped the pillow behind my head. "I know he would

137

want me to spend the money on others less fortunate. I'm sure some river of milk-kindness runs through him somewhere deep inside."

He bent to tug my wet hiking boots and damp blue socks from my feet. I was speechless. My adrenaline-driven energy was washed through and had gone. I was drained. I attempted to roll to my side. I frowned and pulled my knees toward my chest. I, pointing to the parcel of clothes and said in a weak voice, "The money…". But I could say no more. My eyes were closing. Now I knew how the Englishman could sleep without effort, and I slipped off to sleep after thinking that Kimmy would like Wolf.

CHAPTER 18

A GERMAN WOLF

I peeked through half-opened eyes, not recognizing my surroundings. I directed my gaze to the windows where victorious sunshine broke in between the slats of the shutters forming a wall to wall shimmering ladder laid across the carpeted room. I smiled at the morning and closed my eyes to catch the last traces of a dream or remembrance of the filmy curtains being pulled across the window, and a kiss on my forehead.

In the night, serous fluid had seeped from my raw eyebrow and facial abrasions, drying and crusting the left side of my face to the pillowcase. My awakening smile flashed to a grimace of pain as I tried to peel my cheek from the pillow. Wincing, I quit the idea of supporting my weight on my left elbow, while attempting to push myself up from the mattress. "Ow! That shoulder isn't working." I grabbed the headboard for leverage with my right hand and willed my feet to the floor to accomplish a standard sitting position. "Phew, no mean task." I caught my breath then looked around the strange, unfamiliar hotel room, noting my socks hanging on the wooden, chair back. My boots with their tangled leather laces were collapsed in on themselves, and were flopped on their sides under the wicker seat.

Memory seeped in. Oh, Wolfgang! I don't remember him leaving. When, how did I get into the bed under the covers? I covered my eyes to hone in on last night's detail. He'd closed the shutters and left his business card on the table next to the bed. I lifted the card and saw he'd written the word, "Kismet" on its back. Strange. Funny.

Then, my memory crescendoed back, almost with kettle drums and French horns for accompaniment, replaying yesterday like an incredible action movie. I asked myself if that was only yesterday. I celebrated in a loud voice. "Yes. Yesterday! Hurray, today is 2-6-98! I outlived 2-5-98. It's dead and gone and I'm alive. I'd been wrong about what the numbers predicted. Thank God, it's over." My heart felt light. My head celebrated.

I also remembered with annoyance that Wolfgang had requested a doctor to see me and no one had come. Or I slept right through his visit. "Nah. He never came!" I tried to stand but fell right back to sitting. I gasped and almost fainted. Taking two slow breaths to recover, I geriatrically inched my way to standing and launched into a few painful, mincing steps to the bathroom. Once in front of the bathroom sink, I raised my cut eyebrow and leaned into the mirror. I gaped at my reflection. I flipped on the light to address my swollen-shut left eye, no different in size and color from a ripe damson plumb. "What a beauty I am. But I'm happier than ever." I'd survived!

Unable to smile, but able to purse my lips, I cooed, "Ohhh," at discovering a packet containing a small toothbrush and tiny tube of toothpaste. Getting back to business with great effort, I squeezed toothpaste onto my brush, but had difficulty opening my mouth to accommodate the toothbrush. With slow and deliberate movements, my arm screamed the whole time, I brushed my teeth. I licked away the drop of blood at the corner of my lips and attempted to drink and rinse my mouth.

The thought of Wolf made my lips stretch to crack with a smile. "Ouch, ouch." I chuckled to myself at how I'd come to ride with Wolfgang, how he'd put me to bed and how smitten he was with me. I sighed, not unlike a love struck eighteen-year-old.

I leaned in for a closer look at my reflection, tracing the scratches Asi had left on my face. I considered that the little prince had almost killed me.

My two angels cranked up a new debate. "Did I honestly think I'd die?"

"I must have thought so, because I went to a lot of trouble to prepare to die, if you ask me. And look at how surprised and happy I am to still be among the living today." Both debaters shrugged. An impasse.

My lip was scabbed. Neck was sore. The little Indian lad had left bright bruises on my neck imprinting his frightful desperation. I petted my tender breast bone where Asi's shoes had landed a few powerful kicks. I wonder if an x-ray would show any hairline fractures. Ohhh, what's the difference? I'll heal up.

I wondered how Asi had slept last night, and wondered if that horrible scene would replay in his beautiful head for the rest of his life. "Oh I hope not, poor, tiny fella." I pondered the fate of the grandfather. Had he escaped? He should have. I'd seen the boats pushing off from the shore, to the rescue, if they'd gotten to the bus in time. I was satisfied with my conclusion.

I needed to call Lily. She'll be annoyed I was half-right about my numbers, but she'll mock me, anyway. After the journey back and forth to the bathroom, I eased myself onto the bed with a loud, "Ooofff." I sat and rubbed the aching bruises on my left hip and upper leg, additional proof of Asi's protestation. "Yikes, everything hurts, except for my bullet wound!"

Would Lily and Kim understand that I wasn't ready to return to Pennsylvania? Not yet. Waiting for the hotel operator to assist in my call, I reviewed my life, recounting I'd had perfectly good parents, a husband who didn't beat me, the very best daughter, and wonderful granddaughter, but I'd been floating through life. "I never knew I had Life until yesterday. Now I'm going to DO life. Two-five-ninety-eight was the beginning of my life, not the end!"

Within the minute, I was given the go ahead to speak to the United States. "Gads, this is going to be expensive, but I know Lily's waiting for my call."

After a short interval of some distant clicking and buzzing, the phone at Lily and Stan's bedside rang twice. Before she had a chance to return her "Hello," to me, I broke in. "Lily, oh, Lily, I have such a fantastic story to tell you. You'll never believe it. I did it. I'm alive. I survived 2-5-98."

Lily hollered her greeting back to me, then in an aside to her sleeping husband, "Stan, it's Beverly, calling all the way from India. She sounds so close."

I turned my full attention to the phone, cupping my hands around the receiver and called, "How ARE you?"

She answered, "Wow, you sound like you're right next door. You don't need to shout! Sorry I sound so loggy, but it's after midnight here and we've been in bed for an hour."

I broke away feeling my exhilaration shatter away to shards of unmistakable, cold, hard truth, logic, and shame. "Ah, merde! How could I have been so stupid? I'm sorry, Lily. I forgot about the time change. My head is so rattled from yesterday's accident."

"What accident? Are you okay?" She spoke to me, then to Stan and to me again. I couldn't listen to her because my brain was screaming that the obvious problem was that 2-5-98 was continuing to tick away in the United States. Gray matter synapses clattered in my head. I was unable to absorb the sound of Lily's voice. I pounded my fist on my leg. "Curses! Ouch!"

Lily called, "What, Bev?"

My awareness was laced with benign expletives, "Godzilla! If it's midnight in Pennsylvania, then it's a rip-roaring nine o'clock in San Francisco, and...," I blew out a breath of frustration, and sucking in, reloaded for more verbalized anger. "... Hawaiian vacationers, right this second were cavorting in the damned bright, sunny afternoon surf. Then, even more time needs to elapse before the sun limps around to the International Date Line and calls it a day. Ye gods and little fishes! My thumb strummed across my fingers as I hurriedly counted the hours.

I'm stewed. The damned date won't be over until about, ummm, about 5:30 tonight." My ranting continued. I stopped hearing Lily. I almost screamed, "The damned date is not over yet! What an amateur I am!"

143

I'd looked at a map before leaving Pennsylvania and did the math back then. The self-castigation began. Through gritted teeth, came the following spontaneous poetry, "Shit, shit, merde, ca-ca, and poo-poo, dammit anyway, and fuk-kit! I guess the accident made me forget, but still...

Oh well, dying now will be anticlimactic. Shit!"

Lily heard the background long distance sounds, or the muffled sounds of my muttering and sputtering all the way from India. "Bev, are you still there?" I heard her asking Stan, "I don't know if we're disconnected. I think I hear her, but it's hard to tell. Bev? Bev are you there?" Her sentences were interrupted with clicking. I guess she was tapping the mouthpiece with her finger. "Bev? Bev?"

I wiped my face, and responded. "Yeah, I wanted to let you know I'm fine. Lily? Everybody okay at home? Kimmy? Sara? You and Stan and your grands? My cat? All okay?" Nodding my head, not listening and not hearing her response, I looked to the floor, to the shuttered window and up to the ceiling, saying, "Uh-huh. Good. Good. Well, this is costing a lot, so I'll be talking to you later."

Lily called, "Bev, wait a minute. Your lottery ticket won $500! Isn't that great? You were right about your numbers. Pretty good huh?"

I returned the phone to its cradle, probably leaving Lily standing in her nightgown looking at a phone call gone dead.

I wailed my new mantra, "How could I be so stupid?" I swung my right hand across my chest to reassure my injured shoulder. I whined, "I wish I weren't alone. I'm hungry and my arm doesn't work, and it isn't even damned tomorrow yet."

I spotted the package that Herr Wolf Brucke had handed to me yesterday, before he tucked me into bed. Remembering my agony at trying to sit, then stand from the low bed, I chose to unwrap the parcel from a standing position. I unfolded a wrap-around cotton skirt.

I laughed. He'd chosen a beautiful, Madras print skirt. "Aaahhh, madras, the fabric that enticed me to travel to India. I shrugged at the thought that the city had changed its name to Chennai, but the plaid persisted. A tiny cardboard label on a thread dangled from the waistband, 'one size fits all' printed in English. Herr Brucke also purchased a dark blue, pullover, short sleeved, silky shirt. I approved of the color, seeing it was a perfect match to the blue in the skirt. I shook the brown wrapping paper searching for underwear. "Good God, no underpants and no slip, and he knows it. This should be good." I inhaled in pain as I slid-walked to the bathroom to start water into the tub. "A bath will make me feel better, IF I can lower myself into the water." I pulled back the shower curtain and found not a tub but a shower and a drain in the tiled bathroom floor. "Oh, well. Better than nothing."

With great effort, and doing a poor job of it, I washed away any remnants of the Rose River in satisfactorily hot water. I was too achy to reach my back, but the blood rinsed away. I shampooed with my right hand, my left arm too sore to extend over my head. Ouch. I didn't realize I'd hurt my head too. I pulled my fingers from assessing the new lump on the back of my head.

I had trouble bending forward to soap my legs. I was feeling so alone. Oh well, appropriate for a small shower. I dried, patting away the water beaded on my skin, and made my way to my new clothes. My thoughts raced, I want to call Kimmy but I have no money, no clothes, no pocketbook, no…nuthin. I slid back to the bureau. "Thank God, I still have my soggy belly pack."

My investigation of the damp, silky pouch showed my wrecked passport and intact plastic credit card. Camera and lipstick to be jettisoned. I was sorry to lose all of the photos of the scenery leading up to the tragedy at the Rose River. "Well, I got out with my life." I swiped at a hot tear. "Dammit, how could I be so trite, forgetting the time change. I'm as bad as Phileas Fogg. And he was fictional! What's my excuse? Honestly, this must remain a secret. Stupid, stupid, stupid."

A quiet four-beat knocking at my door was repeated with a firmer, more persistent knocking. I reached for my new wrap-around skirt. I shook the skirt open with my good hand and eased it over my head to land on my shoulders. It flared around me like a blue and purple print material cape covering me down to my upper legs. Most of my spottily washed, naked body was covered. With finger tips, I gingerly brushed my hand back and forth through my short hair, again celebrating the no-work hairdo.

Wolfgang Brucke stood at the other side of my door, balancing a tray with one hand as his other hand, knotted into a tight fist, narrowly missed knocking into my face when I opened the door. We both laughed at the close call.

He presented two cups of coffee and a large white cloth napkin over a plate, hiding what I hoped was breakfast.

"Frau Sch…, Mrs. Schuler, how are you this morning? Oh I see your bruised face now matches the skirt you haff around your shoulders."

My mouth fell open. My lip cracked. I was pleased with his frank energy, familiarity and outright good humor. He closed the door with his foot then carried the tray to the bureau.

"Mrs. Schuler, I present some delightful Indian pastry, filled with honey and nuts. Delicious. It's my favorite Indian food. Here also, coconut milk rice, nice and warm and good for a lady viss bruises. And cherries. You will think they look like cherries." He bent forward and made an exaggerated flourish with the white napkin. "Then we must go. I have a plan for you." Turning to me he continued, "All the people and all the baggages were removed from the bus, and your things, your luggage is now inside the depot building. After we finish this breakfast I shall drive you to reclaim your belongings. Then I will take you to the clinic, then you will come to recover at the home of my family. You shall be our guest, and in a day or two, you will have your balloon ride. First, we must claim your luggage and dry out your clothes."

"Oh, thank you, Mr. Brucke. All of my luggage? Oh, what a gift and a relief. I was feeling rather sorry for myself. I suppose everything is soaked; some items will be beyond repair, but what a lucky thing for me the bags have been retrieved. Will you drive the Englishman back to claim his property too?" I embarrassed myself at how I couldn't stop talking. What an idiot.

"No indeed. My dear purple lady, I am taking you alone. Also, the Rose River depot is where I pick up my next Balloon Adventure customers. I must see if anyone else has arrived for a balloon ride. Anyway, you are a customer who finds herself without her coverings, and we cannot have that. We Germans," he said as he poked his thumb into his khaki shirted chest, "are an efficient people and we must get your garments, your clothes." He delivered the patriotic speech, thick with accent and a broad smile.

"Oh, how can I thank you enough?" I trilled. I sounded like a vacuous teenager.

"Drink the coffee while it is still hot," he suggested, leaning toward me, holding out the cup. What did the doctor say when he came last night?"

With effort I extended my hand to take the drink. My face pinched in pain. "No doctor came. But, I'm well enough to be quite hungry. Thank you for the breakfast. If my money is still in my luggage, then I will repay you for the hotel and food." I swallowed a gulp of coffee and said, "The coffee tastes so good. Phew. Hot, but good." My jaw ached when I opened my lips far enough to take a good sized bite of the pastry. "Ummm, the honey is so sweet. But it hurts to chew," My hand came to my cheek as proof.

"My poor lady. You are hurt more than you recognized yesterday."

Coming closer for a better look, he asked, "Don't you remember coming to the hotel last evening? Remember me paying the clerk to get you a doctor?"

"Yes, I remember, but no doctor ever showed. Maybe I slept through him or her banging on my door. I slept like the dead. No surprise."

"I'll talk to someone at the hotel desk about no doctor coming to see you."

I smoothed the makeshift robe around my neck and said, "You mentioned the people were taken out of the bus. When you said "taken" off, did you mean they were helped off the bus, or were they … did they survive, or …?"

"I can't say."

I listened, again running his commentary through the translation lobe of my brain. "I have not seen any newspaper this morning other than the Indian language paper. Sometimes we do not learn the end of the story. I do not have any more details, other than a barge hit the bridge. I got my information by calling the depot. I wanted to know how long it would be before the bridge would be open to traffic. In two, three more days is the answer." I left Wolfgang sitting at the table, swinging his leg and sipping coffee, as I excused myself to dress in my new clothes. The skirt slid down to my waist, but I had difficulty in raising my injured left arm above my head to drop the blouse to my shoulders and over my breasts. I fussed and groaned and grumbled before coming to the obvious conclusion. I inched to the bathroom door, my bare back to the bedroom. "Mr. Brucke? This is awkward for me to ask, but you've been such a gentleman, yet I need one more favor."

"Ja, indeed my fine lady." He walked to the bathroom door, and discreetly turned his shoulder away, insuring my privacy.

"I ahhh, I ahhh, please help." I bit my already sore lip. "I need help. Could you please help me to pull this new blouse over my head? My sore arms aren't working." He hid a smile and rolled his eyes. He held the blouse, and not leaning over for a gratuitous look, turned his head to the side as he eased the shirt over my head to my shoulders. I guided the material over my breasts and smoothed the blouse to my waist. When the job was done, I turned around and met his big eyed expression. Silence followed as we breathed the same air and pretended no intimacy had happened.

Wolf said a jolly, "Well!"

I looked to my brown stained boots, and groaned when I bent to retrieve them. "Thank you. That was intense." We both laughed.

Wolf looked to his own feet. "Don't worry about shoes for today. We can now get you some strap shoes in one of the stores."

"Sandals?" I asked.

"Ja, strap shoes." No further questions.

After I finished every crumb of pastry, and every little fruit resembling cherries, we set off to reclaim my soaked property. Wolf gathered up my belly pack. "Here, you carry your boots. That will explain to any hotel guest why you are bare feets." I shuffled along to keep up with him.

At the check-out desk, Wolf Brucke was disappointed to learn the large sum of money he had paid the desk clerk last night, for the doctor who was supposed to see me, was not accounted for, and not available for refund. No one knew about money for a doctor or even that the American woman required a doctor.

I produced my credit card and paid for the room and phone call as the German's neck and face pinked. He muttered in his native language as he assisted me from the hotel, across the sidewalk and into his vehicle. My blank expression returned him to English. "Now to the clinic for a quick 'see-look.' Then to the depot, then to my home for full recovery."

"Oh, Herr Brucke, except for achiness, I'm fine this morning. I can't tell you how happy I am, and in general, am in love with life today." Yikes did I say, 'in love' in front of this guy? I was embarrassed and turned my head to the window. Would he misinterpret that last remark? I was steadfast in denying that I needed medical attention. I sat in the front seat and stretched my legs, almost. "But, I would like those shoes you mentioned."

Wolf answered. "Yes, Ma'am." He then bragged, "My daughter is a nurse,…"

I stopped hearing his words to process he'd had a daughter. The voice in my head intruded. Of course he has a child. He's about my age, give or take a year.

"…and she'll be happy to look at your injuries later today. We'll go now, to retrieve your baggages. Mrs. Schuler, I am so sorry for your sad experience yesterday, but I must confess to being ferry happy at this chance to meet you. Do you know the word 'kismet?' I think this is kismet, yes? And yet I should be ashamed to say such a thing to a woman I met chust yesterday."

I could think of no appropriate answer. I ran my hand through my brushy short hair again, remembering this time to avoid the tender bumps, turned my bruised face to the window and smiled. I enjoyed how he pronounced, *"Ch-ermans"and"Ch-ust."*

"Please call me Bev. My name is Beverly Schuler. But you already know that from my balloon trip confirmation." I felt silly introducing myself after, well, after him probably seeing my breasts. I thought this man was indeed a genuine Prince Goodheart. My cracked lips reminded me not to smile so widely. Tasting blood, I licked my lips clean and turned my eyes from his face.

Wolfgang laughed, "Again, please call me Volf."

I subdued a swoon. I considered perhaps I was feeling faint, and so swept away because of being in a foreign country, like a movie version of a damsel in distress. But what explained the outright blushing? I had to admit, he was a handsome man. I further supposed he was over six feet tall. Very nice.

His thick sideburns and the receding hair at his temples were the only evidence of white on his head. He brushed his hair straight back, in a Franz Liszt look, or another handsome, caped, debonair legend from days of old. He was so European. Why hadn't I noticed yesterday how good looking he was? I concluded I'd been in shock.

Speeding out of Chennai, I thought I saw the Englishman, now in shoes, standing on a street corner among the throng of locals. I pointed toward him and called, "Oh, look, it's your British friend." Having called attention to the salesman, I slid down below the dashboard to hide from sight. "I would hate for him to see us tearing out of the city together while he tries to hail a cab."

I got the giggles when Wolf looked down on me, ducked over, hiding from the Englishman. I said, "I'm laughing now, but for the life of me, I don't know how I'll get out of this position. I'm so sore and bruised." Despite the laughter I was thinking I still had to survive another eight hours of 2-5-98.

CHAPTER 19

RECOVERY and MEMORY

The sun baked the breeze to stillness. The Jeep's engine was the single sound on the road. Wolf and I rode in silence. I comforted my left arm with absentminded stroking as I looked over the landscape of short hills and trees. Wolf's eyes were hidden behind his dark glasses although his lips were pursed in a tuneless, whistling pucker. He caught me looking at him and smiled a toothy smile. I shot my hand to cover my plumy eye and directed my gaze to my new sandals.

"Thanks so much, Mr. Br ... Wolf, for getting me these sandals. They're wonderful, and when I get back to Pennsylvania, if anyone compliments them, I'll tell them they were purchased for me by a guardian angel. My hiking boots are way past their prime. I smiled my best, half-injured-face smile at him.

"Vell, it's all business. As soon as you have collected on your balloon ride, I shall dump you on the edge of the city." His lips returned to whistling.

After half-an-hour's ride, we joined a road choked with trucks, several cars, and a colorfully painted bus.

I said, "I can't believe my eyes. What's going on?"

Wolfgang speculated, "I think all this traffic is being turned around because the Rose River Bridge is still…ahhh, not able to pass — impassable? The depot is about five kilometers ahead. My business is on this side of the river. We'll see."

Arriving at the depot in another half an hour, he helped me from the front seat, then walked into the building to see if any balloon customers were waiting. I squinted against the punishing sunlight at the scene of sad quietude. An oppressive air added weight to the atmosphere that engulfed the site of yesterday's bridge accident. Bewildered people milled about with their bundles and suitcases, waiting for rides. Spotty shade provided by a line of olive trees provided a good viewing platform where clusters of people sat, picking at lunches, peering toward the river. I glanced at four men in turbans crouched beside a canvas-topped truck backed up to the rear of the whitewashed bus depot. My hand went to my throat in worry that this truck might contain drowned people.

I followed Wolf into the building, past two rows of long benches facing a gated counter where bus tickets could be purchased. A familiar Pepsi dispensing machine glowed from an otherwise empty wall. A large round clock ticked away above the open door to the pebbled earth's parking area. Wolf and I were directed to a back room, created by a too short drapery on a thin rope strung across a larger room to provide a dividing wall. Two tables held luggage and a waterlogged mountain of other recovered parcels. My backpack and shoulder bag slumped against each other like two rejected prunes on a cutting board. The purple fabric had been compromised in the muddy water. The English salesman's briefcase lay flat with weeds dangling from the handle. There was nothing of the bus driver.

My giddy joy at recovering my property was tempered by seeing the brown, paper-wrapped packages the women from the back of the bus had had with them. Rips in the paper still secured in uncut string, showed pastel cloth now stained. I wondered why the women had not reclaimed their property. I rationalized they could be recovering at their homes, and would be back later to receive their packages. Perhaps they lived too far away or maybe it was too early for the others to return to the scene as Wolf had. Maybe they'd never be back. I attempted to scoop up my belongings, but discovered I was unable to lift my luggage.

"My dear lady, you go sit on a bench under a tree. I'll collect your things."

I turned to leave but stopped. "Wolf, would you please ask what happened to the grandfather? His hat and shoes are right over there." I pointed, looking around with dull eyes. And please ask about all the women, too." I pushed the drapery aside, passed the few customers sitting on the benches and left the building. I slip-walked down the dry pebble strewn incline toward the river.

Yesterday I had stood right here, exactly here, on these brown pebbles. Asi's parents comforted their child and rebuffed me. Rebuffed was a kind word. I reasoned their reaction was normal. They must have been frantic when they saw their son's bus careen and explode off the bridge into a river. Yesterday, 2-5-98.

I stopped, emitted a shrill intake of breath. The drowned bus remained with its tail end poked up. The back door of the bus was open, responding to the waves, opening slowly, closing slowly, a foot above the water line. Rowboats holding one or two men each floated near the bus. They gesticulated and called to one another, although I could not hear them. I noticed a man closest to the back of the bus shaking his head "no," in answer to a language I could not understand.

I staggered backwards and fell to sitting on the uneven soil of the river bank. "Ooof!" I petted my aching left shoulder and upper arm, then swiped at the tears that rolled over my fingertips. My forehead touched my knees and I cried. Thoughts streamed … those women in their beautiful saris … were having so much fun … the grandfather … so loving … Dear God

I watched the water. Yesterday prayers would still not come, but now the beseeching words spilled straight to God in heaven. "Please, let them be alive, please, be alive, please, and well."

Three brown boys in shorts and bare chests kicked up sand and stones as they ran past me. The tallest of the three swiped at and yanked a spindly branch from a bush as he ran down the incline. The boys' bare feet were inured to the hurt of the pebbles as they raced to the water's edge. They crouched down, busying themselves slapping and worrying the water as they pointed toward the bus. The leader of the threesome spanked the skeletal wood on the brown water, splashing a spray of diamond glitter each time the branch lifted from the river. They pointed and stood in a close, safe camaraderie.

No fishermen were in evidence today. More bad luck plagued the Rose River. A barge, close to the bus, held a turned over crane, lying on its side, dangling its broken arm partly in the water, partly in the mud, looking like a useless, dead praying mantis with its many angles, a failed attempt at retrieving the bus.

"Missus?" A beat of silence, then the greeting repeated.

I lifted my head and sniffed, blinking my watery eyes at a strange, young man. "Missus, may I help you to stand?"

I nodded agreement and offered my good arm. He assisted me to my scrambling feet. The suited man looked familiar and spoke a beautiful British accented English. "Madam, I came to look for you today. I am Asi's father."

Although he continued speaking, I stopped listening when he mentioned Asi. I interrupted, "Oh, you're Asi's father? How is he? And how is the older man?" My fingers came up to my mouth as I regretted the question, afraid to hear the answer.

"My son is well and is now in the hungry arms of his mother. His older brothers have not yet forgiven him for having a greater adventure than they ever hope to experience. Plus, Asi received from you a 'lucky' silver moose. He thinks it's a holy Brahmin bull." He hid a half smile.

"The older man is my father-in-law, now in hospital, 'being watched,' as they say. He was upset, of course, being part of the accident, seeing the horror and fearing for his grandson's life. He's still weak and disoriented, but he should grow stronger with time. He'll be medicated and pampered for a few days.

"Madam, I want to thank and reward you for your self-lessness. And I apologize for not thanking you yesterday." He reached into his jacket's chest pocket, his smiling eyes thanking me.

I saw the move toward his monetary plan, shot out my good hand, splayed my fingers and blurted, "Oh, no. Yesterday after the bus hit the water, your father-in-law pushed Asi into my arms and, well, there was no time for discussion." I explained why I couldn't take money for a natural response that was its own reward. After a bit of back and forth, Asi's father kissed my hand, bowed and returned to his handsome vehicle, parked next to the depot.

Wolfgang, and Asi's father nodded to one another as they passed on the river bank. Wolf joined me at the water's edge. I stared back at the river. Without talking, he shook open a large, blue, bandana he had purchased in the depot. He pulled and crumbled the paper label, *Made in India*, from the corner of the material. "Here Mrs. Shu…. Bevff, let me help that poor arm of yours." Wolf turned me to face away from him, and smoothed the material, now folded into a triangle across my chest. He hummed a tune as he folded the homemade sling up across my left arm and tied a knot behind my neck. Obliged to stand still, I told the story of meeting Asi's father, and how he'd attempted to reward me.

I patted the sling, smiling at the relief to my aching left arm. "Thank you, Wolf. This feels good." I looked away, avoiding his eyes. This was the most I'd been touched by any human in the last two years. And I thought I hadn't

160

cared about intimacy and closeness. His breath on the skin of my neck, as he tied the knot, raised duck bumps on my arms. I shivered.

Wolf finished his task and turned me around to face him. Seeing the tears on my face, he took a step back to size-up the situation. His hands cradled my face. "Oh my dear lady, did I hurt you viss my made-up bandana thing here on your arm?"

I faked being uninjured, and surreptitiously rubbed my eyes with my right hand. I blinked at the sun, pretending there were no tears. I smiled at the man, but was altogether weak from revisiting the scene of the horrible accident. I was overcome again with the deep sadness at the sight of the bus in the river, and the memory of those women in their saris, standing with the deepening water swirling around them. Relieved to have reclaimed my luggage, I followed Mr. Brucke, who lugged my shoulder bag and backpack, took my good hand, and led me to the Jeep. "Come on, my lady. We have no one to take back to the balloon ride today, so you and I shall eat, and then we shall look at your bruises."

CHAPTER 20

A HACIENDA in INDIA

Wolf's property was ringed by a high, vine-covered concrete wall. His Jeep rumbled through open gates, under a wrought iron arch. I admired a rambling low building with a sign hanging from a wooden post advertising Das Bruder Brucke Ballons.

Wolfgang braked to a dusty stop under a short tree in full leaf next to the long, low porch in front of the ranch house. Pebbles sprayed up against the undercarriage of the Jeep. "We're home," Wolf sang out in a tolerable singing voice.

I nodded. Gosh, the place looks like a hacienda. I guess if the design is right for the heat of Texas or Mexico, then it's good for India, too. I had not thought about what sort of house this man would live in, but all the same, I was surprised by what I saw.

Here I was, in India, meeting a German man who lived in a Mexican hacienda, but instead of a split rail fence, this house and yard was surrounded by a high stone and concrete wall. I might have awakened from a dream. How did I get here? Yesterday I was swimming to save Asi and myself, and today, I was in a new life. I whispered, "And, except for the tragedy I brought with me, I am happy to be here."

I further admitted to myself I was half in puppy love with this handsome man."

The German plucked his cowboy handkerchief from his back pocket and clapped the blue and white material to his nose and mouth to avoid breathing in the clay colored dust raised by the tires. Walking around the Jeep to open my door, he wind-milled his arms to clear the air.

A picture perfect basset hound arrived at Wolf's feet. "This is Dieskau," he laughed, touching the head of the happy canine family member who ran in a large circle like a circus dog. "You know the German lieder singer? Fischer-Dieskau?"

"Yes, I sure do." I leaned down and patted the happy dog's head. "*Wie geht's, Dieskau.*" My smile created wincing pain from my injured cheek and puffy eye.

"He's a dog who howls. And so, with apologies to the master singer, we named him for that famous German baritone, you call it?" I enjoyed this man's sense of humor.

"Please come along, Mrs. Schuler. Right this way." We kicked up dust as we walked the blue-black flagstone path to the front porch. Wolf dropped my sodden luggage to the porch floor. I grieved that the remaining bags of M&Ms would be wrecked. Oh well, they'd been free. Easy come.

Dieskau stayed on the flagstones to investigate the river-soaked bags.

Leading me through the low front door Wolf called in German, "Anybody home?" He took my good arm and led me into a kitchen, bright with midday sunshine. "Welcome to the home of Das Bruder Brucke Ballons. My brother, Hans, the other Brucke Bruder, painted the sign you see here. He is by far the most best artist, but I AM by far the most best looking. Good?" He delivered the line with a wicked wink. "My daughter is here to make you welcome. Take a seat here so your arm can rest on the table. How's that homemade…" He searched for the word, pointing to his arm and shoulder in a sweeping motion.

"Sling," I offered.

"Ja, how's your sling?" He turned from me to lean into the shadowed hall, calling, "Gisella, Gisella, are you here? I haff company. Come and meet the lady I told you about yesterday, the lady who saved the child. Gisella, are you here?"

A young woman, who appeared to be a year or two older than Kimmy, followed by a nine-year-old daughter, hurried into the kitchen. Wolfgang did the introductions in German then in English. We women bobbed our heads in greeting. Gisella's English was flawless. Her single braid hung to her mid back. A wispy crown of yellow curls touched her forehead.

Wofgang continued, "This beauty is my daughter, Gisella Rajanathan. She used to be a Cherman girl, but now she is an Indian wife. She helps the rest of us to fit in here in Chennai."

Gisella punched her dad's arm, then greeted me in English.

With great relief, I relaxed into my mother tongue. "Your dad bragged about you. He says he could not do without you. And he tells me you're a nurse."

Wolfgang proudly placed his arm around me and said in German to his blond daughter, the female version of himself, "This is my next wife, Gisella. She was so brave yesterday. You should have seen her."

Gisella smiled with her mouth, but not her eyes. She spoke to him in German. I think I understood, "Daddy, you are embarrassing me. You met her *YESTERDAY*." Anyway, that was the flavor of the conversation and it is exactly what I'd say to my father if he met a woman yesterday and called her his next wife one day later.

Wolf returned, "Gisella, she almost died. She saved the life of the four-year-old. I believe he is a child of the Singh family."

The German language was strung through with English. I got that I was alone and out of my country. I got that Wolf liked me, now that he was getting to know me. I laughed when he said I had the best quality of the Yanks, and when we met, my eye had not yet bloomed into a ripe plum. He said in English, perhaps thinking he was still speaking in German, "She's quite beautiful." Then turning to look at me, he said in English, "I apologize for speaking Cherman, but when I speak to my daughter, my mother tongue chust flows."

Bending to eye level with the girl, who stood twisting the black tip of her pigtail, I put my fingers under the child's chin and said in English, "And what is this pretty young lady's name?"

"Oh, this is my most best granddaughter, Liesel," Wolf crowed. "We speak Cherman to her at home, but she learns some pretty good English at school."

With all eyes on her, Liesel blurted her German question to her mother, "Why does Poppy like her? She's ugly." Again, I got the gist.

Gisella cried out a loud, embarrassed laugh, "Oh Liesel, I hope Frau Bev does not understand German."

Gisella threw her arms around her daughter as if to smother her, and to push the words back in. The young mother's face flushed to a cotton candy pink. Liesel knew she was in trouble but did not know why. She crinkled her eyes shut and opened her mouth to a loud bawl. Tears sprang straight off her cheeks.

I turned my face to hide my purple, bruised face from Liesel. "I'm scaring her."

Wolf responded in authority, "Nonsense." He bent down, placing a large hand on Liesel's head, saying soothing words to her. Gisella echoed her father's words, not letting the child off the hook for her rude remark.

Pushing a cup and saucer toward her guest, Gisella invited, "Here Mrs. Schuler, have some tea and sandwiches. Father said you would need food when you arrived. After you have eaten, I will show you to the guest room. Father also wanted me to have a look at your injuries."

Hans, the slightly taller, artist brother, entered the kitchen from the garden, wiping his hands on a soiled cloth. He looked like Wolf, but was balding. He had the same square face with blue eyes, but had deeper creases around his eyes. Gisella jumped from her chair and said, "Oh Uncle Hans, this is Mrs. Schuler from Pennsylvania. She'll be staying with us while she recovers from yesterday's accident."

Uncle Hans clicked his heels together and bowed, took my hand, looked into my good eye and said, "How do you do?" The question started with a long aspirate 'h' followed by well-formed words.

I swept my hand to my face to cover the bruises and said, "I'm embarrassed to look like this, but your brother decided to pluck me from the Rose River yesterday."

The handsome basset loped into the kitchen on the heels of Hans. The dog was not one to miss out on excitement, nor the possibility of a dropped morsel of food. His tail wagged so loudly against the floor as to not be ignored. Hans acknowledged the dog, begging for attention. "You've already met Dieskau?" I nodded.

Wolf leaned to pet the velvety head of Dieskau. He looked to his brother, "Ja, Hans." Wolf started a stream of fluid German, as they both looked at my bruises at the same time and nodded in sympathy. Hans shook his head and said, "Tsk-tsk," at intervals with his hand wrapped around his chin.

I figured this was the part of the story where the bus's nose was submerged, or perhaps Wolf was retelling of when the parents grabbed the child from my arms. Hans had a serious face as he regarded this injured American seated at the family table. I understood the occasional word, but watched Gisella's face mirroring her uncle's and father's expressions.

Wolf's eyes scanned my bruises and stopped at the five sutures in my upper arm. "Ach, the sewing stitches in your arm. Oh, my poor, dear lady." He bent to my shoulder to, "Kiss it, make it better."

Duck bumps shot up my arm. I brought my head to my shoulder. "Oh those!" I touched the knotted thread. "That was quite a story—for another time. But, they're ready to come out." I looked to Gisella. "Are you the kind of a nurse who can remove stitches?"

Gisella bent in for a look, clucked, and agreed she could and would remove the sutures, but later.

Hans again bowed to me, "Well, Missus, I shall see you again. Good-bye for now." Each word was polished like an individual apple. Hans tugged Liesel's pigtail to her playful wail as he exited. Dieskau followed.

Wolf scraped his chair to the table, knocking his knees into mine. I yipped and squeezed my eyes closed. He blurted a German apology. He looked to Gisella for her best translation of his awkward English.

"Dad seems to be so smitten with you. He's behaving as I have never seen before." Gisella laughed, setting a sugar bowl and a honey jar within my reach.

Addressing her father, she handed him a stack of letters, saying that this was the mail for today. Wolf placed the stack of letters on the table. I stole a glance at the address on the letters, not knowing what to hope for. Force of habit. I saw the house numbers were not 2598. I exhaled a quiet puff of air.

Wolf, the purported handsomest Brucke bruder, poured a glass of milk for himself and Liesel, then pointed at the envelopes with his square fingers. "You see these numbers? 4238? Isn't it a funny coincidence, my house number is the same as my birsday?"

169

I had my cup of tea halfway to my mouth, but clattered the cup to the table. "You are kidding? Did you make that up?" Hot tea splashed my face. I ignored it. Three hands with napkins met and dabbed at the spreading pool. I looked at Gisella and said, "Are you serious? Gisella, is he telling the truth? Is your house number the same as your dad's birthday?"

"Yes, Ma'am, it is. I have the same thing." Gisella reached for a tea towel and finished the drying, shining the table top. "Here, let me give you more tea." She inspected my cup, no cracks or chips, then filled it again.

Gisella smiled, and winked at her father, "I have some recurring numbers, like Poppa, though they're not my birthday digits. My lucky number is 23. I found out I was accepted into Columbia University in New York on the 23rd of the month, I received a twenty-three-hundred-dollar scholarship, I had room 23 in the off-campus housing, oh, it goes on and on. My husband, Hari and I were married when I was 23, on the 23rd, and of course, the stork brought Liesel on the 23rd of November. So, 23 is my lucky number."

I sat with my mouth open wide enough to fit in a pomegranate. "I can't believe it. I'm here because of my special numbers, 2598. And I don't know if they're *good* lucky. The jury is still out on that one. Yesterday's date was 2-5-98 when the big accident happened."

Wolf broke in, "Dear Mrs. Bevfferly Schuler, from now on, 2-5-98 will be the happy date I met you. And the lucky day you saved the life of a lucky child. So, all is ferry good. Ferry good. Now let's eat this lunch and have no more worry."

Hans returned to the kitchen table. He wiped machine oil from his hands with a chamois. "Wolf, I forgot to ask where you put the key to the..." His question was interrupted when Dieskau followed his master into the kitchen, livening up the gathering. The smiling basset arrived carrying a flat-as-a-dried-leather-shoe, dusty, dead, brown rodent. The quiet domesticity was over. The women and child clustered together at the far end of the kitchen pointing and calling in various languages, "No, no, bad dog!" Wolf ran to grab Dieskau's collar and pulled the culprit from the kitchen. Dieskau dropped his prize and looked from face to face, full of pride, searching for approval. He thumped his heavy tail into a chair's leg. The two men's lower voices called over the higher pitched women's instruction of where the dog should be and who should retrieve Dieskau's donation. Hans grabbed the dead rat with his chamois as Wolf escorted the dog outside to the flagstones.

Liesel dashed from the kitchen as soon as someone mentioned the German words, "dead rat." After the dog situation was resolved, Gisella stood up, holding her sides with laughter.

After a lunch of a few meat and pickle sandwiches, Gisella led me into the sewing room cluttered with fabrics strewn across the single guest bed. Seeing the fabrics reminded me of the soaked, string tied packages waiting at the Rose River depot. The sewing machine stood open. My attention was brought back to Gisella's sunny sewing room with her gasping an apology about forgetting the guest room was still torn apart. She straightened, organized, and replaced the vase of glass tulips to the now closed sewing machine's top, and at last, led me to the bed, pulled the spread down, and patted the spot for me to sit.

"Let me examine your injuries. I'm sure you're healing up well, based on how vertically you jumped up from the table when Dieskau arrived with his prized dead rat. But, I need to quiet Papa's worry about you."

Gisella gave me a thorough going over and wound up with a sad "oooh," at my black and blue swellings that she carefully avoided touching. She ran to the bathroom closet and returned with a bottle of alcohol and vigorously scrubbed the scissors she'd scooped from the sewing basket. She held my left arm and said, "You can watch or look away. In any case, this will be easy." After a few snips of the threads that had been part of me since Alaska, Gisella placed a dab of antibiotic grease on the site and topped it with a bright orange child's bandage. "That was easy. I feel like a famous surgeon."

My hostess proved to be a good, doting mother. She patted my head and maternally kissed my forehead, and backing up with a laugh, she knocked over a framed photo. "Oh, poor Mutti." The photo clattered to the floor.

Gisella recovered the picture, and holding it, sat next to me on the bed. "This is my mother and me in Denmark the summer before she died. We had so much fun on that vacation." Gisella smiled and caressed the photo with her finger. "I was twenty-two. The next year I went to New York to study at Columbia, but I've already mentioned that."

I nodded, not asking why Wolf's wife died. Gisella smoothed the blanket and bedspread, and stacked the now folded fabrics on a book case.

"Mutti died of breast cancer. It's why we traveled to India. My parents tried every possible cure in Germany, and in Europe. She died too soon after coming to Chennai." Gisella smiled, looking at me, then indicated with her head toward the bed, "Okay, you're all set."

I spread my hands on the mattress to prepare for lying back. I winced as I eased backwards on the bed. Lying flat, I blew air from my cheeks. "Sitting used to be quite an easy thing."

Dieskau showed up one more time, but without a donation. Gisella clapped her hands to get the dog's attention. "Come on Dieskau. We'll give Mrs. Schuler a chance to sleep. Pleasant dreams."

I curled up on my side, sparing every achy body part, closed my eyes and enjoying the comfortable bed, was off to a long restful nap. When I next awakened, the date throughout the world would be 2-6-98. At last!

CHAPTER 21

HELLO to ROMANCE

I awakened to bird song. I listened. "How different this concert was from the commotion the birds made outside my window on the morning of the accident." I lay flat on my back and considered how far I'd come in the nine days since I'd met Mr. Wolfgang Brucke. I rolled over in bed, noting almost no pain anywhere. Alaska's stitches were long gone, my sling was folded in a tight triangle in the bottom of my back pack, my bruised ribs were fine, my sternum, sporting a pale green smear, was the single remnant of Asi's rescue. "Pain free — wahooo!" My hand brushed across my face for a new morning's report of my puffy eye.

"Kismet," he called it. I smiled at the ceiling and twisted a finger through my hair that was by now almost long enough to hold a curl. I still had not had a balloon ride, and was not eager for it. Sooner or later I'd have to decide what was next. My family, at last, had stopped asking when I was coming home.

I needed to decide if there was a Wolf Brucke thing going on, although he seemed to think so. I'd give him the right idea if I stuck around any longer. I needed more time. More time to be away. More time to decide where I'd go next. What was next? Kimmy's exact words to me on my last call to Pennsylvania were, "Being 'in love,' you should pardon the expression, is way inappropriate at your age, Mom."

Like a teenager, I rolled to my stomach, kicked my feet, pounded my fists into the bed and muffled a stress relieving scream into the pillow. My door creaked open. I lifted my head from the pillow. There was Wolf peeking around the door. He was bent over, sneaking in. I snapped to sitting bolt upright, not bothering to pull the sheet to my chin. I was thirty years past worrying if another adult saw my bare shoulders.

Wolf whispered, "Vell, good morning Miss Eyes vis Sand." He smiled.

I returned the smile. Where did he get his expressions? The origin was obvious, but what he missed in translation was comic.

"Hi ya, Wolf. *Wie geht's?*" I smiled at what I could not hide. Ahhh, his delightful bass voice and his wonderful accent. I was melting.

Wolf sat at the foot of my bed, my feet scooting over to give him room. He took my hand. He was easier to understand today, or was I becoming accustomed to his accent?

"I have a confession to make to you. I, of course brought you here to help you recover and to give you our famous Bruder Brucke Ballon ride."

I nodded, smiling at the top of his full head of salt and sand colored hair as he bowed his head to talk to me.

"Mrs. Bevfferly Schuler, I'm afraid if I take you for the balloon ride I owe you, you will have no reason to stay here with me. So, what would you like to do? I am not quite ready to let you go."

"Good question, Mr. Wolfgang Brucke." I reflected his mock formal style. I dug down to my school teacher, acting voice. "I have overstayed my visit. I'm well enough to travel, although, I'm not ready to go back to my own insignificant life in Pennsylvania. No burned bridges, because I'm too busy seeing the world. I still have sufficient finances to go on to Vietnam or Bangkok, and, or somewhere, anywhere. Those visits could be on my way home, but I'm still not quite ready to go home. I haven't considered my next step because of my injuries. I'm healthy enough now to consider moving on. And, I'm keeping this lovely hostess from using her sewing room. In the U.S. we say guests are like fish, they stink after three days. It's time for me to go."

"Do you *want* to go?" he asked sliding up the mattress toward me. He slid his hand behind my head. Looking right into my eyes, he said, "I'm warning you. I'm about to kiss you."

My eyes widened, then crossed as I watched his face come closer and closer to mine. My mouth was already open in readiness to answer him, but instead of talking, I received, then returned a kiss that would have buckled my knees, had I not already been sitting. His weight on mine pushed me back into the pillow. When the delicious kiss was over, he lifted himself and looked at my face. Eyes locked.

Silence.

More silence. I licked my lips and said, "Mmmm, very nice."

My heart was pounding. Wolf's face lost its smile. He pulled himself to a proper upright sitting posture on the edge of my bed. He looked into my eyes. I likewise sat up, and rubbed my hand across my uninjured head to straighten any hair in need of correction. Wolf plopped his hands on his knees, punctuating the silence. He turned to me and we both nervously laughed.

We jolted with the sudden, "Oh, hello Poppy," that Liesel sang out in German from the open door. She smiled at finding her grandfather, and entered the room, holding a gift-wrapped packet close to her chest.

Wolf and I laughed again at the surprise. He squeezed my hand. He responded to his granddaughter. "Yes, my little dolly. How are you this morning and what are you carrying?"

Liesel could not have known what she had interrupted. Holding out an offering wrapped in tissue paper, she announced she'd made a gift for Miss Bev. Wolfgang translated, and pulled Liesel up to the bed. I received the gift and peeled back the tape to not tear the paper while the child leaned against my arm for a closer look.

As I included the proud child in opening the gift, Gisella arrived in the room. "So this is where the party is. I've been looking for you. Breakfast is almost ready. Why have I been left out of the festivities?"

I held out a black, rolled shoestring strung through a thin clay disk decorated with seeds and a few chips of broken colored glass. "Oh, Liesel, *es ist sehr schon.*" Then to Gisella, "I hope I said, 'it's beautiful.'"

Liesel smiled and bounced up and down. Gisella's head bobbed side to side to show the translation was close enough.

"Well, Mrs. Bev, the *jewel* was Liesel's idea." She reached to hug her daughter.

Wolf interrupted, "Ladies, as pleasant as this gathering is, I was having a word with our guest." He shooed Gisella and Liesel from the room. Patting me on my poked-up knees, he said, "How about you ride with me back to the Rose River today. I have a group of passengers who are expecting me at two o'clock. Good?"

Wolf bent and kissed my forehead followed by a whispered remark about 'Frau Graulich.' Huh? Who's Frau Graulich? I'd ask him later. He was sixty, so of course he'd been with other women after the death of his wife. I wondered how I stacked up against this Frau Graulich.

Wolf's eyes peered straight ahead as his hands held the steering wheel at the two and ten o'clock position. We rode in silence. My knees were pulled to my chin, my feet on the seat. We squinted into the sunlit expanse ahead of us as dust blew up around us. Wolf broke the silence, "Bevfferly, I may have to stop this truck to kiss you again. What happened earlier was not quite enough. Yet, I must remember, you could arrest me for kidnapping you." His face was deadly serious.

I laughed aloud. "Oh, get out of here. You can't mean that."

He interrupted, "Bevff, you were injured, almost in shock, you were in a foreign country with no money."

I couldn't resist. "And no underpants!"

He continued, not picking up my playful line. "I took advantage of all those things. I brought you to my house without asking your permission. I have not offered you a chance to leave. I have kept you to myself. I have directed all conversation away from you leaving." He pulled the truck into the shade of a highway overpass. He reached his arm to me and pulled me close to him.

"Come over here, Mrs. Bevfferly Schuler. You are altogether too far from me."

I laughed and without any more encouragement slid right under his arm with my chin up, looking into his face. He faced up to his task and turned off the ignition and kissed me soundly. Again, I offered no resistance. I hummed a high swooning tune when the kiss ended. He slipped his hand down my back and under my blouse at my waist. An involuntary sound chirped from my lips.

"Wolfgang, I haven't had any skin contact in over two years since my husband died, and who knows for how much longer before he died. I need to be ready. But not yet."

"To be honest, I vas not going to compromise your wirtue here under this bridge, but I might like to put in an order for some time in the near future. Good?"

I blew air out from my pursed lips. "Well, you understand I would like that, but first, I'll have to ask my mother for permission."

Wolf straightened up and gave the key in the ignition a twist. The motor revved. He said, "You hear that motor? That's how I feel. Vrooommm. Vrooommm. Mrs. Schuler, watch out." He moved the truck back to the road but kept a hold of my hand.

I, like the implied girlfriend I was, slid over to him, shoulder to shoulder, hip to hip, like teens.

Back at the Rose River depot, Wolfgang went into the building. He parked in the same shady spot where he'd parked on the day of the accident. I hopped from my seat and walked to the road's edge where I could look across the bridge to the far side of the river bank. The doomed bridge I'd traveled almost two weeks ago now supported vehicles that were being squeezed to the right lane, alternating right of way after every five or six cars. A new barge was in the water at the broken bridge support. The yellow bus was nowhere to be seen. The tipped over crane was also gone. The scene was as I'd seen it before the accident. Boys and the same black dog were at the water's edge. A few men on the bank fished. I supposed the choppy water from all of the rowboats between the barge and the shore would dissuade the fish for coming up to nibble at the fisher's bait.

Wolf called. I enjoyed hearing my name with the ff sound at the end of Bevff. Ah, this might turn out to be love, I mused.

He had with him the Tanakis, a family of four. Wolf introduced me to the customers as a lady who might be included in the balloon ride because I had missed the opportunity nine days ago. The senior Tanakis who appeared to be in their late sixties, were on an extended trip to celebrate their forty-fifth wedding anniversary, sponsored by their dutiful son, who stood to the side, his feet tight together, his hands folded. He executed a shallow bow on his introduction. A grandson, Michael, aged twelve, was along for his own betterment and to keep his dad company. The grandson was forbidden by his mother, the younger Mrs. Tanaki, who continued to rule from Hawaii, to go on the balloon ride. All piled into the Jeep. Wolf phoned Gisella to tell her to expect four customers for lunch and to contact Hans to get the large basket ready for a four o'clock launch.

Gisella had a buffet lunch set out on the house's spreading front porch. The Tanakis helped themselves to the bottles of a fruit drink wedged in a round bucket filled with large chunks of ice. A pitcher of dark tea sweated with the midday heat. Bananas were heaped with small melons and pineapples as a center piece. A bowl of rice with shrimp, lemon slices, red pimento, and black and green olives dominated the table and was the hands-down favorite of the family. The Germans and I pecked away at the fanned arrangement of cheese and ham slices. *Dinklebrot,* with mustard and butter in clay jars were protected from flies and bugs by a large, square gauze umbrella covering the food.

Dieskau, genially supervised from knee level, skirted the picnic table, recognizing an opportunity for dropped cheese, meat or bread. Michael, not permitted to have a dog at home in Hawaii, spent most of his time bent in half talking to the dog and seeing to the occasional meaty favor to Dieskau.

After lunch Liesel signaled for Michael to help her pull the propane tanks from under the tarps in the garage. For a girl who spoke German, some Tamil, and elementary school English, she was easily understood by Michael as she pulled at him, pointed, and led the way. They lifted tanks to the ground at the doors of the trailer. Liesel lined the tanks in a semi-circle on the grass then indicated for Michael to follow. Wolf would check the tanks and load them himself.

Uncle Hans had painted artful and colorful striped balloons on both sides of the silver trailer. Liesel had Michael's attention. She pointed to Uncle Hans, and in elaborate sign language, indicated it was he who had painted the picture and words," "Das Bruder Brucke Ballons on the trailer." Michael agreed with good humor, nodding his understanding. "Uh-huh, uh-huh."

I watched Liesel pull coils of rope from the wall of the garage and pointed for Michael to load them into the basket, already in the silver trailer. Liesel was directed by Uncle Hans to collect the new fire extinguisher from the back of the Jeep. The kids went into the silver trailer and pushed against the gondola, and the generator. All was set out, counted again, pistons rechecked, ropes checked for tangles, and tanks re-checked for volume.

Uncle Hans was on duty as always for the last minute check of the counting and to review the work Liesel did for each outing. He lugged a bag filled with bottled water, salty pretzels, a few tangerines and chocolate bars to the floor of the Jeep. Hans had his walkie-talkie attached to his belt. Wolf had his. Hans handed out candy bars and thanked the kids in English and German for a job well done. After the balloon was launched, Liesel and Michael would join Uncle Hans driving the "chase" vehicle.

If Michael was disappointed in not flying in the balloon, he gave no sign. I busied myself with Gisella in collecting the shards of lunch. "This looks like the end of the 'sermon on the mount.' Only a few pieces of bread and some crumbs are left. I guess we were all starved, or you're a good cook, Gisella."

She laughed. "Gosh, yes, Poppa pretty much finished up the watermelon and the pineapple. We feed the customers, but this family ate better than most."

"Do your balloon customers ever get airsick?" I stood holding a stack of scraped dishes.

Gisella called her answer over the noise of the hot water rushing into the kitchen sink. "No. There's so much to see. It's pretty amazing." She took the plates. "I think you'll love it. The launch is short, no time to get sick. The whole thing, coming and going takes about three hours. You'll be back home before dark. And Poppa carries salty food, crackers or pretzels if the customer feels, ahhh, feels woozy. Is woozy a word?" I nodded. We laughed.

While carrying the last of the fruit drinks into the kitchen, Gisella turned to me. "Bev, you'd better get ready if you are going with Poppa and the others today."

"Going? In the basket, or in the Jeep?"

"Well, that was an interesting question," Gisella said. She put her elbow on the sink's counter and propped her chin on her fist, and waited for a more detailed explanation. Her eyes drilled into mine. "I thought your whole trip to Chennai was to go on a balloon ride. So today's your chance."

"Uhhh," I stalled. "I'm not sure there's room for me today."

Gisella frowned and shook her head "Don't be silly. There's room for six in the gondola Poppa has loaded and ready to go." Gisella swung an arm around my shoulder. "Bev, are you afraid? Is there some problem I don't know about?"

I was embarrassed and tangled my fingers. Tears filled my eyes. "Gisella, when your dad kissed me, well, he, uhhh, he,…"

Gisella stopped her work and stood straight to hear this tearful confession from her father's new girlfriend. "Kissed you?"

I looked across the walls and the floor with wet eyes. "Yes. Well, who is Frau Graulich?"

"Frau Graulich?" Gisella's voice asked in a high pitch. "Didn't daddy tell you who is Frau Graulich?" She didn't wait for my reply but turned and shot from the kitchen. I stood alone and wished I were not crying.

I watched Gisella catch up with her father by the trailer. She commandeered him from his work by grabbing his collar. Wolf dropped the coil of rope and followed Gisella's emergent pace toward the kitchen.

I did not know what was said between them until several weeks later, but this is how it was described to me. "Poppa, Bev is worried about going in the balloon. You must have said something to her about Frau Graulich because she is worried." He stood with upturned palms and shrugged his shoulders.

Gisella answered his gesture. "How am I supposed to know? You need to talk to Bev, and now." She pointed to the house. "She's pretty upset."

This is where I was present. Wolfgang came to the kitchen twisting his cap in his hands. "Bevff, is there a problem?"

I turned to him and went weak in my knees. I sank into a kitchen chair. Wolf grabbed my arms. "Whooooah. What's happened to you, my dear lady?"

Hans was calling from the driveway. He needed Wolf's help in attaching the trailer to the Jeep. Gisella ran to Uncle Hans to tell him there was a problem brewing in the kitchen. The Hawaiians gathered at the picnic table, smoking and making nervous small talk. Gisella played the hostess for a while, keeping the guests at ease while her dad did damage control in the kitchen.

I choked out, "Wolf, I know it's foolish of me, but I'm afraid about my numbers and our future. My future. I know it's crazy, but I have what you have with your birthday and your house number and what Gisella has with her number, twenty-three. Do you understand? And not the least of it is my having no excuse to stay after the balloon ride is over. Will you want me to stay? Should I go, continue my planned vacation? Go to the Orient? Go back home? These are the ridiculous things keeping me from going today."

Hans arrived on the porch, slapping dust from his pant legs. Gisella was standing near the open door. Hans patted his niece's shoulder, and seeing his brother, the senior pilot in the kitchen, started to walk inside. Gisella grabbed his arm and pulled him back. Before Hans got the story unfolding in the kitchen he called, "Wolf, I called the Kingsley brothers. They'll meet us at the launch." Wolfgang turned to look back over his shoulder at his brother and daughter standing a respectful distance on the other side of the door. He heard Hans's remark, but was distracted by his immediate, more pressing problem. He said, "Ja," and closed the door on their faces. He swung his arms around me and lifted me to my feet.

"Mrs. Schuler, it has all been decided. It's kismet. Yes? You will marry me. You will marry me, yes? Not today, Mrs. Schuler, not today, because today we are hurrying to have a balloon ride before the sun sets. But soon, because your numbers brought you to me. I love your numbers and I love you. Now, if being planned and promised to me today makes you want to ride with me and the Hawaiians, then my heart will fly with me. Otherwise, if you want to marry me but want to stay here with Gisella, then I will rush home to you today. I loved you when I saw you walking out of the muddy river with that desperate boy hanging on to your neck. I loved you the next morning when I saw your eye like a plum. These are things I should tell you like a lover sitting on a blanket under the moon, but I am now racing against the weather report and winds most best to ballooning. Did I say that right? You may kiss me now and we'll have to make this all official after you tell me how you were loving me too from when you first saw me. Good?"

He smiled and planted a welcome kiss on my surprised mouth. I kept my eyes open as I looked over his head in question at how the events had unfolded so quickly. Two minutes ago I was carrying food into the kitchen. One minute ago I was expressing my doubt out loud to Gisella, and this minute I was kissing my official boyfriend. Beyond a boyfriend, Wolf was now my fiancé.

I sighed. I don't know who you are, but Frau Graulich, take a number and get in line.

CHAPTER 22

THE BALLOON and the BUTTON

The two kids and Wolf squeezed into the Jeep's front seat with Uncle Hans. The three adult Tanakis slid left to make room for me to climb into the back seat. Hans rumbled the Jeep eight miles from the hacienda. He made a remark about not having enough elbow room to turn the Jeep's steering wheel. The fun had begun.

Wolf turned to the adults in the back seat as the vehicle bounced across a narrow bridge, "This is a thread of the Rose River where Mrs. Schuler was baptized a few weeks ago." He smiled at me. He slid his hand back between the seat and the front door and let his fingers linger on my ankle. If the Hawaiians had any question of who Mrs. Schuler was to the company of Das Bruder Brucke, the picture became a little clearer, manifested by the sidelong look Mrs. T. gave to her sexagenarian husband. Michael and Liesel squashed arm to arm, ignored each other until our parade passed the dusty, dried carcass of a long dead hyena.

Michael called, "Ohhh, look." He nudged Liesel who pouted and rubbed her upper arm. She made a face of distaste at the sight of the skeletal animal, grimaced, said a translatable, "Yechhh." Then she returned a punch to the boy's arm.

Wolf witnessed the event and laughed, calling a German remark to Hans. All I could understand was, "*jung liebe.*"

Within twenty minutes Hans pulled over to a pile of rocks on an otherwise flat piece of dusty, scrubby ground. The Kingsley brothers, two British college students in Chennai often earned money crewing for Wolf and Hans. They popped from their car and met the ballooning party. Each called greetings to one another and hopped to his task. Liesel and her servant, Michael, helped to unload. The Hawaiians enjoyed their supervised job of pulling and unrolling the blue and purple striped tarp of the balloon, all being careful to not step on the Dacron. Side vents of the balloon were examined. The senior Mr. Tanaki laughed and talked and talked, full of nervous energy as he worked.

Mrs. Tanaki mosied out to a heap of rocks and settled herself. Silhouetted in the sun, she lit up a cigarette, turned her face to the warmth of the sun and exhaled a long stream of smoke. Wolf watched in disbelief. He dropped the bag of bottled water and snacks, and ignoring the bottles rolling away, he jogged to where she sat. My view of the silent drama was of Mrs. Tanaki looking up at Wolf standing over her, flinging his arms. I hope he remembered to speak English. His arms said, … lit cigarette … wind … bottled gas, and flames! She shook her head and gestured with her hand to apologize, pressing out the cigarette, then tapped herself on the head to apologize for her dunder-headedness. Wolf, quite the mime, backed away.

The kids jumped into the silver trailer and pushed as the junior Mr. Tanaki helped Wolf and Hans and the Kingsleys rock the gondola from the trailer. Like slaves pulling the pharaoh's blocks of stone, they put their backs into moving the basket to a clear distance from the trailer. Mrs. Tanaki, now without a cigarette, still seated on the pile of rocks made notes in her tablet.

The men attached the flattened, purple Dacron to the basket, now lying on its side. A large fan was situated between the basket and the balloon where the generated wind blew directly into the balloon's mouth. I gathered the renegade bottles of water from under the vehicle's tires and returned them to the food basket. At the boss's order, I obeyed and pulled the Jeep around to the other side of the rocks to put some distance between the lift off and the Jeep's overhead frame. Michael stayed busy following Liesel's pointed directions. Wolf jogged twenty feet back to the Jeep and pulled a small tank of helium from under a blanket. He inflated and knotted a child's red party balloon. At his arm's length, he released the little helium balloon to be carried off, indicating the direction of the wind. When I returned to the group Hans was testing the gas jets with twists of the valves. I brought my hand to my nose and mouth, and burped, trying to not vomit from the gas fumes.

Wolf noticed my green tinged expression. "Darling Mrs. Schuler, are you all right?"

"Well, I think it's the fumes from the gas. I'm a real success out here, huh? I'll buck up before long."

At last, the customers and pilots walked back to the Jeep to relax while the generator powered fan blew air into the belly of the balloon. Everyone jolted to attention when the balloon billowed in a sudden, snapped loud rip, forming a huge, upright purple and blue bulb. A volley of applause and explosive laughs came from the congregation. The fan continued to blow air, now spinning dirt, grit and stones, stinging our faces, and eyes. Liesel ran to the basket's side to cut-off the power to the fan. Uncle Hans nodded at his niece, thanking her for her quick work. Balloon up, pilots to their feet.

Wolf dumped the basket of snacks and water bottles into the gondola, waving his free arm to the Tanakis to join him and get aboard. The men climbed indecorously over the four-foot-high rattan rim and hoisted Mrs. Tanaki into the basket, depositing her next to her husband. Inside the basket were rattan support walls running from side to side, dividing the gondola into four compartments, separating the fliers, room for two in each compartment. Wolf waved and called over the sound of the jets for me to hurry and climb in. I stood with my eyes shielded from the sun, and did not respond to his instructions. He called again, reaching for me. Unknown to him, I had not yet decided if I was in or out. Liesel came to the rescue and unabashedly pushed against my buttocks and me toward the basket. I screamed at the surprise of being attacked from the rear, reminiscent of the Brahmin bull. Hans, the dutiful brother, took advantage of my vulnerability, scooped me up, and dumped me into the gondola.

I screamed again and held on to the inside compartment for stability. The basket bumped across the ground again, then again. Wolf called to Hans and the kids, "We'll see you

192

in about twelve miles." He laughed, reached up to the balloon's mouth and pulled the tab to release more flame and heat into the proud, puffed out, purple envelope. I glanced at Wolf, then realized I was looking down on Liesel's and Michael's happy faces as they waved up to us.

Hans ran to the Jeep followed by the kids. All jumped in and the Jeep powered into the west. The Kingsley boys, likewise, hustled to their car and followed Hans. I looked at my watch. The time was 5:05, no numerals with a remote tie to my or Wolf's lucky numbers. I chastised myself. I'd become a crazy woman, always checking for those darned numbers. I'd have to get over this weird number stuff. Period.

Mrs. Tanaki kept her hand on her husband's shoulder, pointing to folds and risings in the geography below. As close as she was to me, I couldn't hear their conversation. Mr. T., white faced, stared straight down. He pulled his wife's body to him, pressing her back close to his chest, and gripped his hands around her waist. They faced in the same direction, her head touching his cheek. Their son felt the shift of position of the reedy and rubber matted floor and looked to his parents to scold them for jiggling the basket, then he looked away from their intimate posture. He looked up, down, then out at the thin, far away wisps of cloud.

Wolf could not reach me from my place against the far wall, so sent a quick cheek shifting wink. He pointed in large, dramatic gesticulations, indicating what he wanted me to see, and what he'd later describe. I peeked over the side at Wolf's hollering and pointing, and nodded, "uh-huh, uh-huh." My hands were fisted at my chest. Did I look terrified? I wrapped my hands around my upper arms in a warming gesture. "Should have brought a sweater," I called to Mrs. Tanaki.

She called back, "The brochure said we would not need one."

I answered, "I think I'm a little scared. Maybe that's what made me shiver."

Mrs. Tanaki pointed her thumb over her shoulder toward her husband and called, "Well, you can see who pulled me close. You weren't the only one who was a worried." We smiled at one another, and raised our knowing eyebrows.

I looked straight up into the colorful stripes, noting how the light played from outside the balloon, wildly iridescent at the widest diameter and deeper color at its narrow throat. A purple stripe reflected across the Tanakis' faces, lighting them in a surreal color. I stretched to move closer to the edge of the gondola to look at the landscape. Wow! No wonder God loves us. Look how beautiful earth is. Rust on a truck, or the hyena carcass could not be seen from this height. Imperfections did not show. In the distance behind the balloon, like toys below, I watched the one-inch Jeep and the college kids' half-inch car in line following the balloon's direction.

Everything was beautiful. The greens looked washed and the trees look trimmed, all even and tidy. The patterns on the earth look like artwork. This is beautiful. Oh, there's the Rose River. How innocent it looks from here. I wish Kimmy could see this. I looked at Wolf and threw a bold kiss and yelled, "*Danke, Herr Brucke.*" He laughed and tugged on a vent strap.

A sudden gust bossed and bumped the envelope, causing the gondola to buck and tip. All passengers let out a, "Whoa," in unison as the large bag recovered and floated obediently to Wolf's maneuvering. The jolt caused Mr. T's hand to come up to his head in a protective movement, knocking his camera from his shirt pocket. The camera flipped into my space, hit the floor of the basket. I bent forward to snag the camera as it had tumbled near my feet. As I attempted to straighten up, I felt my rear pocket tugging me backwards. In an awkward posture, knees bent, doubled at the waist, I reached behind myself, touching the basket. My pants button was caught in the weave of the rattan. I couldn't move forward and I couldn't stand up straight. With no one noticing my dilemma, or dismissing my posture as not unusual, my button agreed to slip downwards to the next cross reed, allowing me to inch myself down to a crouching posture. Still, no one noticed. I mumbled, "Oh, good God, I'm freezing, nauseated from the damned gas, and bent over facing the floor. In general, this is a wonderful first balloon ride. I'll make the perfect wife for someone whose lifework this is." I pocketed Mr. Tanaki's camera, and swore to myself and wiped away a few indulgent tears. Wolf kept the ride smooth, opening the vent, sending up jets of the gas to sail higher to catch a westward windstream.

After forty minutes of floating, the balloon neared an obvious destination of smooth ground. Wolfgang pulled a rope handle to open the "cork" atop the balloon. Hot air escaped and the balloon rocked, descending as the deflating bulb allowed Wolf to coax the monster to a gentle end of the ride.

Hans rocked his speeding, weaving vehicle between scrubby bushes and short, stony formations to catch up to our projected destination. The Kingsleys, adept in the chase, were close behind. Our balloon's looming shadow darkened Liesel, Michael, and Hans as they hopped from the Jeep. Hans hollered for the kids to stay clear of the basket.

Despite that I was crouched down, I felt the balloon's controlled drop in my head and stomach. Wolf's full attention was on a safe landing. No legal actions to follow. He called over his shoulder to the Tanakis, "Don't worry, everything is good. This is like giving birth. The last seconds are fast and important. But all things work out happily. Hold on tight." His English was perfect.

Without the sun shining through the expanded Dacron, the balloon was now a dark, inverted, brooding eggplant slipping from the sky. Wolf pitched the guide rope from the top of the basket. The Kingsleys and Hans ran to the dangling rope and pulled, not unlike pulling a huge kite behind as they directed the balloon toward the ground. They coaxed the passenger heavy basket and retired balloon to the flat land, not ten feet from where Hans had parked the truck and trailer. The basket bumped and slid to a scudding stop. The Kingsleys ran, hanging on to the basket, pulling backwards to keep us passengers from tipping forward. The exuberant balloon seemed to be reluctant to be flattened and folded away. Hans hooked and weighted the dangling ropes.

As with every trip before, the vehicle and balloon reunited before the sun disappeared behind the horizon. Wolf was first to leap from the gondola, followed by

Michael's father. The seniors required help to climb out, with especial care to the Mrs. to retain her feminine dignity. After the Tanakis vacated the basket, busy with words of praise for the ride, they gathered near the Jeep.

As I worked feverishly at my danged busted button stuck in the rattan, I was able to watch through the weave of the rattan, but could hear better than I could see. What had been a relaxing view of the world had become an emergent event.

I watched Wolf deliver his deep theatrical bow with a sweep of his hat, to the end of another customer satisfied balloon ride. I presumed Wolf was unaware of my dilemma.

Michael's dad turned away from his parents' side to meet his son. He kicked up the dusty ground walking in wide steps, calling to Michael, reporting that the son would have loved the experience and there would be a balloon ride in his future.

Wolfgang hollered to Liesel to reach for "this" or to Michael to run to get the "that" when I saw him stop and turn around, looking for me. The last time he remembered seeing me, he later reported, I was crouching inside the basket. Wolf walked toward the gondola, hollering, "Bevff? Bevff?"

I squeaked a weak, "Wolf, I'm right here." He leaned in to see his newly betrothed, crouching in the basket wearing only a shirt and jaunty red Bikini panties. I was barefooted with my sandals kicked away. I faced the rattan wall, muttering, struggling and tugging my slacks up and down trying to free the stupid back pocket button from the weave. He heard my oaths through my teeth.

197

"Bevff Schuler, why no trousers? Oh my darling woman, you need help."

"Oh hell, I almost had it." I swore. Wolf leaned in, and in a moment the button agreed to let go, and I was able to return to my slacks and sandals. I stood straight after about twenty minutes of crouching in the basket and redressed. I looked at Wolf's face and laughed. At last I was appropriately attired. I patted the pocketed camera and said, "Let's eat."

Gisella arrived in her own car to meet the balloon crew and the Tanakis. She brought sparkling drinks for the kids and champagne for the adults. The bag of pretzels and cookies were opened for the traditional post flight toast. Wolf swung his arm around my shoulders, and we joined the happy, chattering group. I smiled and handed the culprit camera to the senior Mr. Tanaki. His eyebrows lifted in surprise, unaware the camera had fallen from his pocket. He excused, "I was too absorbed in the flight to remember to take photos."

The Tanaki's interrupted each other with joyful reliving of the event. "Michael, birds flew under us ... The air was cooler ... a little ... No, I didn't feel the least bit airsick. The wind moves the floor around a bit ... That's crazy! It's so quiet, floating around, unless Herr Wolfgang is sending more heat up into the balloon, then there is a loud swishing sound ... Mr. Brucke, do balloons bump into each other when there are many in the air ... like the picture of all the balloons crowded together, like on your brochure? ... Why is there always a champagne toast afterwards?"

After the folded, and packaged striped Dacron was expertly fitted into the basket, all the king's men: the hired, the owner, the kids and clients, retired.

The enjoyment of the flight continued into the ride back to the hacienda. Mr. and Mrs. Tanaki had decidedly relit old embers during the flight and spoke to one another. Michael and his dad compared stories of their separate experiences. Hans whistled as he drove. Liesel's eyes closed as she leaned against her granddad's arm. Wolf wedged himself sideways for a worshipful view of his intended, me. I returned the adoration and smiled sleepily, hugging the few unopened water bottles on my lap.

CHAPTER 23

THE SÉANCE

I sat at Gisella's kitchen table, lazily circling my spoon in the fragrant tea. The open door framed Wolf as he walked toward the hacienda. I watched him coming closer until his beautiful shape filled the doorway. I smiled at his dark silhouette, backlit by the midday sun.

He was right on time for our homemade séance. Seeing me at the table he apologized, "I admit this is crazy, but I think a little ghost chasing is chust what we need here." He turned to the counter and picked up a few strips of paper, stacked next to the phone for messages. "Here, we'll need to write our special numbers on these papers."

I slid the strips of paper to the center of the table. "I agree. The other day I was annoyed with myself for checking my ticket, or whatever the hell it was, for my numbers. I felt so childish and yearned for peace of mind. Let's chase those ghosts."

Wolfgang asked, "So, you are all right with the plan?" I nodded.

"Good. Where are the girls?" Wolf approached me, his new fiancée. My heart clanged around in my chest. I held my breath. Lightly leaning on my shoulder, his finger brushed my cheek as he leaned over to place a jar of honey within my reach. "Here my friend, have some *honig* for your tea." He licked his sticky finger.

I smiled up to thank him, but wondered why I'd been demoted to "my friend." Only a friend? I dipped into the honey 'char,' as he called it, then watched the steam twisting up from the hot tea to coax the amber glob to succumb to my hot drink.

"Bevff, you're so silent today. Is everything good?"

"Uh–huh, yes, sure." My spoon clinked and clinked, musically. Anxiety was in the air.

He used the excuse of putting the stubby candle in the middle of the table, to lean in closer to me to place a light, discreet kiss on my ear. I pulled my shoulder up to my ear, punctuating the move with a "Wooo! Tickles," and dropped my spoon. I caught Gisella watching from the hall, waiting for a more appropriate moment to enter the kitchen. I pretended she hadn't seen the kiss that hadn't happened. Caught in the act, like a guilty kid, I said, "Oh Wolf, a candle. I guess this is going to be a real séance after all."

Gisella called into the kitchen, "Okay Poppa, here we are." She and Liesel arrived in a flurry of scarf tails and long skirts they kicked with bare feet as they scurried in. Both looked like Halloween gypsies with strings of gaudy beads about their necks. Gisella had undone her braid and allowed her blond hair to cover her shoulders. Liesel had one of her mother's flowered skirts wrapped twice about her flat chest and pinned above her heart with a rose brooch from her mom's jewelry box. The mother and child hung onto each other, giggling.

My eyes widened. I pushed back from the table. "Don't start without me. I'll be right back." I jumped from the table and ran off to the guest room, rooted through my luggage to retrieve the long, silky, green scarf I'd bought in Alaska. I congratulated myself for purchasing the gauzy accessory for 'emergencies,' never guessing the occasion would be a séance. I knotted the material at the nape of my neck, with the streamers trailing down my back. I scooped up Liesel's gift necklace and centered the pendant on my forehead, between my eyebrows. Before peeling out of the sewing room I grabbed two gold colored curtain rings from a heaped shallow dish and clipped them to the scarf near my ears, effecting large loop earrings. I kicked off my "strap shoes" and hurried to the kitchen, joining the conspirators. We women smiled and nodded approval to one another. Liesel clapped her hands and said 'Wooo-weee" when she recognized the jewel I proudly displayed.

Wolf held my chair. "I see we're having quite the official event today." He followed his sentence by opening his eyes wide at Liesel. He bent to look under the table. "I see nossing under this table that might cause knocking, except for six bare feets."

We ladies tittered. Wolf sat. He took a deep breath. I pushed the small stack of papers and the pen toward him. He selected a slip and scrawled 4-2-3-9 in large, square shaped numerals, and handed paper and pen to his daughter. I was nervous. My fingers danced on my own slip of paper on the tabletop as I waited for Gisella to write her numbers. She wrote her digits, dropped the pen, then hopped up to get a saucer from the counter. She closed the kitchen door, darkening the room, then closed the dark green kitchen curtains. The midday sun refused to be shut out, forcing parallel rays to stubbornly push through the curtain's weave, giving the kitchen an eerie green hue.

Wolf pushed a family bible into the center of the table. Liesel pushed a rubbery, blue Smurf doll toward the candle. She smiled, looking up from under her eyelids. Wolf looked to Gisella to explain how a Smurf happened to be in attendance at the séance. She shrugged.

"Mutti, may I light the candle?" Liesel begged.

"Ja, my Liesel," Gisella answered, handing a sputtering match to her daughter, then leaned to the counter to turn off the wall lamp. We all looked around the table at each other's green tinted faces highlighted by the flickering candle.

Wolf took my hand to one side and Gisella's hand on the other. Gisella grabbed up Liesel's cool small hand and ran her thumb across the smooth surface. Liesel offered her other hand to me, closing the circle. I took up the child's hand, and winked at her. The flame smoothed to a tall, glowing jewel. Silence settled.

Wolf cleared his throat. "Let's begin. Maybe a short speech from each of us. I'll start, then Bevff, then Gisella. I don't suppose Liesel has anything to burn from her young life." Wolf took his hands back from us women. He became serious and touched the Bible. "My dear Lord, I do not hope to offend, but want to burn away my numbers because I am becoming super ... super ...,"

"Stitious," I added. "Superstitious."

"Ja, yes, these numbers are plaguing me, dear Lord." He looked around to see three bowed heads. My pendant hung away from my forehead, directly over the table, like a magnetic needle pointing to due north. Wolf lifted his strip of paper. "I am sorry to burn the numbers because they are my birsday numbers, and of course I have always liked them. But, they must go. So that's it." He lit his paper and dropped it, glowing, into the dish. We all watched the edges smoke, then quit in a smoky poof. We sat silently. After a deep breath, he cocked his face to me. His eyebrows said, 'it's your turn.'

"All right, hand me the pen." I looked upwards to the dark, took a deep, shoulder heaving breath. I wrote 2-5-9-8 on the paper, reached the slip to the hungry flame, and dropped the burning paper into the dish. I shook the heat from my fingers. The paper's corners curled in agony, as dried tea leaves twist when drenched in boiling water. I watched the numbers glow then convert to carbon. "I agree. I have always enjoyed how my numbers kept showing up, sort of like a dependable friend. But their reoccurrence is scaring me somewhat, because, I too, am becoming superstitious. I'm always looking for the numbers." I folded my hands on the tabletop and leaned in to supervise my familiar numbers becoming ash. Like Wolf, I took a deep breath, then whispered, "That was sad. More difficult than I thought,"

I turned toward Gisella and passed the invisible gauntlet. The Smurf doll smiled on, his wide-spread fingers making a long, foreboding shadow across the table. Liesel's wide eyes searched each face.

Gisella said, "Well, I seem to be represented by the number 23. Like Poppa and Bev, I like my numbers because they have been friendly. But I'm also beginning to see the numbers as having a life of their own, and I know that is not right. So, I send my numbers into flame to stop them from influencing my rational life." She extended her slip of paper to the fire, now burning low, and allowed the paper to sink to the dish with its immolated relatives.

We all sat back and rejoined hands, smiling and somehow feeling some of the inner peace accomplished from our candlelit service. The whole kitchen exhaled.

Liesel wiggled in her seat, sat back and stretched. Her bare foot whacked into my knee. I erupted a surprised, pained, "Aaahhh," involuntarily squeezing both Liesel's and Wolf's hands.

Liesel shook her hand from mine, yelling, "Owww!" and jumped from her kitchen chair that clattered backwards to the slate floor.

I likewise jumped up. Startled, Wolf pushed back from the table in a sudden move, his chair screeching a painful protest. Gisella blew out the candle, and watched the séance's unraveling. She ran to open the door. Warm, comforting sunshine broke in with a silent roar. She swished the green linen curtains back to the window frames. The flowers outside in the window boxes cheerily bobbed in the slight breeze, ignorant of the séance happening on the other side of the glass.

Liesel returned her chair to an upright position and hid behind its tall back. Her eyes wide, she tangled her fingers in her necklaces. Gisella grabbed her daughter's hand and scurried back to bedrooms to kick off the long skirts, scarves, and necklaces.

Wolf reached for me. Grateful for a direction, I took my man's hand and hurried through the door and out to the happy, searing sunlight. I pulled my scarf from my head, shivered and said something unintelligible, akin to "Uhhhhhh." Wolf balled up my scarf and shoved it into his pants pocket. Neither spoke. We hugged and walked out to the wild flowers and the weeds.

CHAPTER 24

THE BAZAAR and NUMBER 18

"Come on, Mrs. Bevfferly Schuler. We're overheating the engine, out here in this hot sun, waiting for you," Wolf called over the noise of the Jeep's engine.

I twirled from the hacienda, closing the door behind me. Smiling and pounding my chest in a 'mea culpa,' I slid into the front seat. Gisella and Liesel returned smiles and waves from the back seat. I was forgiven.

"So sorry to keep you waiting. I'd almost forgotten my camera."

Gisella answered, "You'll need that camera. The bazaar is a great place for photos. It's a little southeast of the city, but worth the ride."

Twenty minutes into the ride, Liesel asked a question in German, sounding in tune and length of sentence, to be the equivalent of the American question, "Are we there yet?"

The answer grumbled from the front seat was the unmistakable retort, "soon." I smiled at my successful assimilation, one more point for high school German. I was satisfied with understanding our progress toward the mid-day bazaar.

On the day of my rescue by Wolf, I'd glimpsed a bazaar, down one of the many narrow streets. Pedicabs and bikes wheeled around the car, gaining access through the bazaar's narrow alleys where larger vehicles could not enter. Today, Wolf parked his vehicle two blocks from where we now walked, among an almost impenetrable throng. Gisella had a woven bag slung over a shoulder, leaving her hands free to shop and to hold onto Liesel. I strapped on my belly pack. No longer in a sling, I had both hands free to slip either one to Wolf's proffered elbow. Wolf kicked dirt from his sandals. He was taking his best girl sightseeing. He leaned to Gisella and said, "We'll meet at the Jeep at three." She agreed and peeled off with Liesel in tow.

Wolf slid his hand across mine where my fingers curled over his arm. "You are looking very mighty pretty good, now that you are all healed up." He leaned down and kissed my temple. "Watch out for ..."

I smiled up at my German man. "Kismet," I told him.

We shouldered into an alley jammed with shoppers and business owners. The crowd was made dense by the narrowness of the alley, sided by open shops, and wares spilling to tables on the street. Are we the only tourists here? I was rudely buffeted by a man inching through on his motor bike, beeping his horn. I pushed backwards to make way for him. I looked up to see buildings rising two and three stories with open windows, open shutters, and small, narrow, fenced patios.

"Oh, Wolf, look up. I guess that's what a jungle looks like." We looked up to green plants snaking over the trellises

210

and railings, creating a dangling canopy of leafy cover running the entire length of the narrow street.

Four alleys converged at a central clearing where the buildings opened to a wide open sky. "All right, decision time," Wolf said. "Down that alley are more shops. Over this way are the snake charmers and more scary things. Greater chances for, ahhh, pick-pocks, or ah, pock-pickets? Pocket-picker? You know what I mean."

"Pickpockets?" I smiled at my German. "Uh-huh, let's do both." The streets narrowed to irregular, twisting paths. I snapped pictures of bolts of material, racks of beads and hand-hammered earrings. I pointed to the open market of food. I pulled Wolf to the table of bottled olives, rings of figs, and bottled oils. "Ummm, doesn't this smell good? Is it the bread? Maybe it's the jars of hummus, or the fruit pastes. I don't even recognize some of these smells."

"Curries," he answered. Five young boys bumped through the crowd, laughing and darting through the tangle of shoppers. They called to one another, seemingly enjoying their part in the bazaar. One boy shot out his hand and grabbed a wrapped stem of strings attached to eight balloons from a store front. Their escape was somewhat hampered by the fact that a bouquet of balloons cannot be hurried. The young thief released the balloons that slowly rose to the lowest balcony and lingered there, a colorful cloud.

Having been jostled by the kids, I felt for my waist pack in an insecure moment. Still there. Oh, but I'd already had my purse snatched on this vacation. I laughed and held tighter to Wolf. Merchants had covered every inch of their wire trellises, with hanging, colorful arrays of local goods:

baskets, purses, rope hammocks, and tourist baseball caps with 'India' or 'Nepal,' or 'Mumbai,' embroidered in English, above the caps' visors. I saw a merchant stretched on a lawn chaise, and another slung in a shallow hammock, both sleeping next to their merchandise. Radio music from the stalls competed with music from other storefronts.

I hollered to Wolf, "How can that man sleep with all this noise going on? The motorbikes are noisy, beeping and honking to bump the pedestrians out of the way." I interrupted my remarks and yipped, leaping forward to avoid being soaked by a pan full of cloudy, putrid, water with fish scales and remnants of fish waste being pitched to the drain in the gutter. Wolf turned around to wipe some of the splash from the back of his leg. We exchanged facial expressions that reflected our distaste for the fishy water, then laughed, no translation necessary.

As we meandered, Wolf took a picture of me slipping my fingers through a folded, tasseled scarf of magenta silk. We ambled, not talking, but leaning on one another, bodies touching from our shoulders to our hips, familiar, sharing a casual intimacy. A light ting-ting-ting tingled as we passed a display of red, green, and gold bells hung on a ten-foot-tall fence.

We rounded a corner where the buildings cast a shadow on the alley, and in general the air felt still and heavy. Fewer merchants displayed sale items. "This feels like a scene from an old movie. Where's Omar Sharif?"

Wolfgang pointed out a crowd gathered around a snake charmer. As the crowd shifted I saw the thin, turbaned man crouched on the ground. His knees poked up like stems of two saplings. He looked like any sketch or cartoon of a snake charmer. I was stunned and pulled Wolf in another direction. "Is that a serious thing, or is he there for the tourists?" He shrugged. I leaned up to his ear, "He gives me an uneasy feeling, let's go." Wolf acquiesced and turned to leave the dark alley. I continued, "When I was planning my trip, my sister chided me with the line, 'are you going to kiss the head of a snake in Nepal?' It's funny, but now that the date has passed, and since we burned the numbers, I'm becoming interested in living again."

"I hope I have somesing to do with that." He squeezed my hand and smiled up at the small square of a turquoise sky.

I grinned and snapped a photo of him looking down on me. "There, just for fun."

Gisella and Liesel came toward us from the crowd in the dark alley. Their speed was a sharp contrast to ours, the seniors' moseying gait. Gisella called, "Papa, come on around this corner. Liesel has some money to spend and she wants to gamble it away on a spinning wheel."

When the crowd in front of a spinning wheel came into view, I said, "Now this looks like a Saint Michael's Church's annual fund-raiser. I can identify with this."

A tall, well combed, dark man with long black lashes and a large neat mustache stood behind a wooden counter with a checkerboard surface. He wore an apron with pockets across the hem line, lumpy with coins. Even numbered squares were colored red, and the odd numbers from one to ninety-nine were painted in black. The man tugged the wheel, with one hand and circled the other in the air inviting the passers-by to place their coins on the checkerboard of numbers. The clacking of the large wheel was barely audible above the voice of the barker and the inhabitants of the bazaar.

Gisella stood behind Liesel as her daughter placed her coin on the red square of number eighteen. The hawker pulled on the wheel after others placed their bets on the red and black squares. Liesel jumped up and down in excitement with her hands crossing to her shoulders, hugging her own chest. To keep the child's feet on the ground, Gisella pressed down on her daughter's shoulders. There was a generalized moan as the losers watched the little girl sweep up the winner's money. Liesel was ecstatic with her handful of coins. Gisella laughed and pocketed her daughter's winnings. The child placed another coin on the checkerboard on eighteen. Wolf leaned to her. He told me he said, "There's not much chance of the number eighteen winning twice in a row, Honey. Try a different number." Liesel frowned at her granddad and pronounced in words I could not understand, but again, the tune told me she whined back, "But it's my lucky number!" Or perhaps, " ... because I want to."

About twenty others gathered at the wheel and placed coins on the squares. Again, last bets were called for, and the wheel was spun into motion. The watchers jabbered good humoredly. The crowd held a collective breath, and again uttered disbelief and annoyance when the wheel stopped at number eighteen. Liesel was almost faint with delight. The tall, dark man frowned at Liesel, then directed his frown to her mother.

Gisella leaned to her daughter's ear and whispered, "Now is my turn." She ignored the hawker's reproach, squeezed her eyes shut, kissed the edge of her coin, then placed it on the black twenty-three. Wolf watched her bet, then squawked, "My dear daughter, you burned the number twenty-three."

"Yes, I know. I'm checking to see if it really died."

I squeezed in for a closer look. The noisy wheel clacked around a few times until slowing to a solid number four. One happy man in the front tapped his chest and muttered to the crowd, a short remark that got a laugh from those close to him. He took his earnings and wove his way out of the crowd, around the corner and out of the alley.

"I guess number twenty-three died." Gisella's eyebrows were up. She appeared to be disappointed.

"Well, okay, let's see if 4238 has died," Wolf said. He placed coins on the red squares marked 42 and 38. Others jostled to place their coins on the board. A short, hefty woman placed a coin next to Wolf's on the 38 square. He held his breath as the wheel of randomly placed digits slowed, passed the 42, passed 13, 06, 59, slowed at 46, 31, and ground to a halt on 82. The number next to 82 was Wolf's number 38. Close, but no cigar! The hawker grinned and scooped the coins to his apron pocket. The woman cried a loud lament. Wolf gave her a coin to stop her crying, and she too disappeared in the crowd.

"Come on, Bev. Play your number." Gisella waved to me. "Prove to yourself your number is a dead duck."

"Oh, Wolf, suppose I win?" I jumped up and down as Liesel had done.

"*Nein, keineswegs.* You can't win, because your number has gone up in smoke. But, go ahead; you can prove it to yourself." He winked and jingled coins in his pocket.

"Okay, all right. Help me with the coins." I fingered through my change purse and produced a few coins and held up my open palm for inspection. "Which one of these is the right denomination?"

He fingered through the heap, and handed two coins to me. I leaned to the board, and placed a coin on 25 and on 98. Wolf moved behind me. He threaded his arms around my body and brushed his thumb beneath my breast. I was so distracted by the flush of heat, I forgot to watch the board. I had no need to watch. A happy patron standing back in the crowd crowed a victory song as he moved forward to collect his winnings from number twelve.

Wolf planted a soft long kiss on me, celebrating my loss. Gisella slapped his arm and said a disapproving, "*Vater!*"

Wolf laughed. "Our numbers are goners, Mrs. Schuler. We need a new plan, and we need to celebrate." We headed back to the Jeep. I swung my beau's hand but held my nose with my other hand. I jumped over smoky, putrid puddles where the street vendor had slung water from jars of yesterday's cut flowers. We screwed up our noses at the stink of the alley and marched toward the Jeep. Wolf and I had our fingers threaded in a firm clasp.

Gisella and Liesel, the victorious, money winning daughter, caught up to us old people.

Liesel asked in German, "What does Granddaddy mean when he says the numbers are dead?"

Wolf translated Gisella's answer. "You were there, at our séance when we burned papers with numbers written on them. Remember? We asked them to stop being our lucky numbers. And today the lucky numbers did not come back. Burning them away worked."

"Do you mean a lucky number that shows up all the time? Like my locker at school and my soccer shirt number were eighteen? Wolf turned around to regard his granddaughter, "Ja, precisely like that, Liesel."

Liesel let out a "whoop" dropped her mother's hand and turned back to the wheel. Gisella chased her daughter, "Honey, come back. We're leaving."

Liesel ran, pushing herself between the people in the bazaar, rounded the corner, and had already placed her coin on the number eighteen when Gisella caught up with her. The hawker frowned at seeing Liesel back again, making one unbroken visor of his two eyebrows. Others had placed their bets, leaving the man no choice but to spin the wheel. As the wheel clacked, the man called to Gisella, "Madam, you must take your child away from here. She is bad for my business. This will be her last time to play." He snorted, twisted his mustache, then turned his face to the noise of the wheel and called for the crowd to gather around. The wheel slowed, 23 ..., 88 ..., slowed, 56 ..., 34 ..., and stopped at eighteen.

Liesel screamed a German 'Yippee' and turned to hug her mom, then jumped around. Gisella put her hand on her bouncing daughter's shoulder to ground her. The man groaned, shifted his weight and pushed the board full of coins to Gisella. She extended her hands for her pay-off. He frowned, "And, Madam, don't come back."

He muttered an obscenity under his breath as the crowd backed from their losing bets, and searched folds in their clothes to yield a coin for the next spin of the wheel.

Gisella and Liesel pushed through the crowd to Wolf and me. Gisella called to her father, "Did you know Liesel's special number is eighteen, and that her bedroom is eighteen paces from our bedroom? Did you know she wore number eighteen in the spelling contest, and did you know her soccer jersey number was eighteen, and did you know, that right now she placed her coin on her lucky number eighteen for her third win? Gisella squinted and counting on her fingers, said, "It's about twenty dollars in American money. The kid has a lucky number, folks."

Wolf looked at my slack expression and said, "I guess we need another séance."

CHAPTER 25

THE WEDDING

July 1998

A summer wedding was chosen to allow the Pennsylvanians to attend. Sara would stay with Liesel. The two little girls would have plenty to discuss, with their wedding dresses to accessorize and Liesel doing all the language translation.

Taking a page from my book, Lily and Stan decided to see India before the wedding, winding up their two-week travel in Chennai. As she put it, "Bevy, why should you have all the fun? No one we know in Pine Bluffs has been to India, so we'll be the first, oh, the second."

Gisella drove me home from the shopping spree. My hand was up to my forehead keeping my longer hair from blowing in my eyes. "You know, I hate to be all bridey, but I kinda like longer hair, to look more like a girl, than my extreme vacationer, mountain climbing, river swimming, Girl Scout look. What the heck, India's bleaching sun has made my brown hair almost as light as my white hair. Blends right in." I gave a wide, goofy smile. My wedding dress, protected in a long, slender paper bag was slung across the back seat of the Jeep. Wedding shoes were in a box on the floor, along with two new outfits I'd be taking on the honeymoon, among the many bags of necessities and gifts I'd bought for

Lily, Kimmy and Sara. I had no gifts for the men. I called over the sound of the wind blowing over the windshield, "The men are on their own."

Gisella laughed. "Don't worry about the men at the wedding. Hari, my wonderful husband, has bought some good beer for them."

"Men suffer through weddings. Too bad the groom has to attend the wedding at all. Seems to me, he should be out drinking with his chums until the wedding is over, then show up after the party to pick up the bride and the gifts. Good idea huh? Whether there's drinking before or after the wedding, the one thing for sure is that there will be drinking. Mainly, men need each other, and beer."

"Ah, it's good for them. Makes them bathe and dress up. Keeps them civilized."

I nodded in agreement and added, "You should have heard my phone call to Kimmy. She tried to stay polite and cool about me being married again. Her father has been dead for two and a half years. I mean, that's more than the standard period of widow's weeds. She doesn't know I mourned our marriage for no fewer than twenty years. I don't think Kimmy has any idea I wasn't happy. Neither did I. My life was so insignificant, even to me. I went on and on without questioning. Wash dishes, tend the garden, pack lunches. That was it."

Keeping her eyes on the road, conveniently avoiding uncomfortable confessional eye contact, Gisella asked, "What does your sister have to say?"

"She's focused on this chance to be in India. I'm so proud of her. Now that I think about it, maybe her annoyance with me for making this trip, was her envy because I was getting out of Pennsylvania."

Gisella nodded in agreement, lips curled in to her teeth, "Probably."

"Kimmy will change her attitude when she meets all of you," I said. "And I'm sure Sara and Liesel are going to manage, even though Liesel is much more sophisticated. She's such a good hostess to me. What a sweetheart.

"Up to now, I've been afraid to face my own family. I'm worried about their condemnation of me for bold facedly choosing happiness. We Pennsylvanians are down to business, and sometimes downright dour. My sister and daughter have been a little cool to me on the phone. I told them to cheer up, because packing for India is easy in the summer. They don't need to pack a lot of bulky clothes they would need if I'd met your dad in Saint Petersburg!

*

My family made the trip to India in July to witness the marriage. Kimmy stood at my elbow, nodded 'yes,' her discreet signal in answer to, "Who gives this woman?" and took the bouquet at the appropriate time in our private ceremony. We were gathered in Gisella's spacious living room. Liesel, now best friends with me, held the lace topped pillow, that moments before held two gold rings. Sara carried a heap of flowers. The girls wore matching, floor length, yellow and white eyelet dresses, dresses provided by Kimmy. The girls were elated. They each had tiny flowers and draping yellow ribbons woven into their long, French braids.

Sara's pale hair and Liesel's thick dark braid put one in mind of Princesses Rose Red and Snow White. The girls were also happy with offering the guests a bowl of M&Ms that had indeed survived the river dunking, thanks to the many plastic bags I'd wrapped them in to ensure they'd better survive India's heat.

Hans, the pretty darned good looking Bruch's Bruder, stood tall in his blue suit at his brother's shoulder as I, the bride presented my rosy lips to the smiling groom for the kiss that sealed our marriage. A spontaneous "Hurrah" went up from the crowd. Kimmy and Kevin, along with Lily and Stan, stood in a semi-circle representing Pennsylvania as Granny Bev, in my turquoise silk, floor length dress, married a balloon man.

The Germans' enthusiasm outshone the Americans' shy demeanors. The guests from India, the smattering of Europeans, and four Asians from Wolf's past teaching days, moved among our families. All were congenial. "T'was a lovely service," said I, the bride.

I watched the aggressively American Sara, elbowing Liesel, getting closer to me, jockeying for my attention. I whispered to Wolf, "I foresee a little rivalry for the grandmother's affection. I don't think Sara is cool with her competition being slightly taller and speaking more languages."

Wolf rose to the occasion. Clapping his hands he called, "Where are my two beautiful nine-year-old girls? Let's get their pictures. It is so wonderful to have one blond, and one black haired granddaughter, like salt and pepper." He fussed, calling the photographer to the task. "Be sure to have many playful poses; standing, leaning, running in the garden, holding flowers, throwing flowers, including Dieskau with his bow tie, and maybe get the girls in the balloon basket." He collared the photographer, "Pictures of the children make everyone happy. Now go." The photographer was inspired and removed the girls from the indoor party. I had to congratulate Wolf for his cleverness and tact.

I had my own spy work to do. I broke away from the guests and wifely demands. My daughter and sister had landed on the same couch, sipping their drinks and sampling colorful, petal-topped canapés. I'd been correct in my summation that I could stand behind the doorpost to hear what they said. I knew the naughtiness of eavesdropping, but rationalized that when you're the bride, it's your day, and everything's legit. I heard some of Kimmy's annoyance with me.

"A new stepfather, at my age!" She continued, to my surprise and entertainment, "Honestly Aunt Lily, I feel like I'm the adult and Mom is the kid. How can she marry a total stranger after fewer than five months of knowing him? I mean he is a nice enough man, and I'll admit that he's rugged and charming, but what kind of business is balloons? It's almost as if she ran off to join the circus, for God's sake."

"Oh, I don't know. I think he has chosen the balloon business. He has plenty of money from what your mom says. I think he can afford her. And, I think he's the one who talked her into marrying him. That's how your mom tells it, anyway." She dabbed her napkin at Kimmy's damp head and neck and straightened her crooked rose corsage, dusting the wayward baby's breath from her niece's dress. I almost flew from my hiding place to explain my own point of view, but was embarrassed at my own, bad, spying behavior, bad, even for the bride.

Lily said, "As you know, your mom and I don't see eye to eye on some things. It's the same with you and your mom, right? Don't you two support each other even though you disagree?" I nodded agreement from behind the doorpost.

She continued, "Mostly? At least in theory? I mean, Stan and I are here to support your mom, even though I don't always agree with her, you know? She told me she's in a rush, because she is afraid she doesn't have much time left to enjoy life."

Kimmy crossed her arms at her waist. She shook her head, "I don't get it. She keeps saying I'm too young to understand. Well, I'm thirty-three, a mother, and I keep Kevin happy," she interrupted herself to wave to her husband who was talking to Stan. "… and have two cars, a mortgage, and in what way don't I qualify as someone who wouldn't understand my own mother? And it's bloody hot in India in July!"

Kimmy quieted and became reflective for a moment. She twirled a flower stem in her fingers and stared ahead. "You know Dad wasn't nice to Mom. She never said or did a thing about it. I'd have left him. He was civil to me but was a bastard to Mom. Interesting, isn't it that she's getting another chance? You're right. I guess I should be happy for her."

I almost orbited with the joy at Kimmy's insight. I started to back away, hoping for a discreet get-away, but stopped when Lily spoke again, "Kimmy, dear niece, your mom didn't ask for our permission for her to marry. She invited us to be here to share the time with her. I think she's crazy, but let's be happy for her. She's right. Her wedding has gotten us all out of Pine Bluffs for a change, and, well, that was a real accomplishment. It's what she wanted. Let's enjoy India." She blew cool air upwards from her jutted lower jaw to her face. I turned away from my listening spot, both arms raised in a touchdown sign, and beaming, caught up with Wolf.

Lily looked past Kimmy and winked at her husband, who was smiling at the magazine beautiful, model looking, Gisella, moving among the guests, offering slender flutes of champagne. Gisella and Lily said "Congratulations" to one another in unison. Hari sat at the piano and pounded out a gusty Bavarian tune. The violinist sawed rosin onto her bow as the flautist shined his instrument with a purple velvet cloth and joined the music making. This was not the first time the three musicians had performed together. Hari called to the violinist who answered with laughter. The flautist's lips were pursed over his mouthpiece, not allowing any rejoinder other than flashing eyes and lines forming on the forehead wrinkled upwards in agreement.

Wolf turned to me, scooped the champagne glass from my hand, swallowed the last of my drink, and placing his right hand to my back, he danced us straight into the center of the living room. The wedding guests cheered and clapped, parting from congenial conversations to make way for the celebrating wedding couple. I put my head on my husband's shoulder. He reciprocated by placing his cheek on my hair, careful to miss the sprig of baby's breath with a few rosettes tucked behind my right ear.

I closed my eyes, Thank you, God. I asked to live longer and perhaps to dance close to a man again. Thank you for my life.

The music turned to a spritely piece. Gisella stood behind Hari at the keyboard, her hands patting the top of his shoulders as she bobbed her head from side to side, in rhythm with his music. Kimmy's husband, Kevin, spoke some German he'd learned while living in Bavaria as a child. He approached Liesel, now back from the photographic session, and asked if she would like to dance. Her face showed surprise that Sara's American father spoke German. She curtsied and took his hands. The adult and child faced each other and took long dancing strides to the left, then happily reversed their dance to the other side of the room. Wolf yelled some cheery remark to his daughter. I understood nothing of it, but Gisella and Liesel had a good laugh. Kimmy looked around the room, shrugged and picked up a child's xylophone from atop the piano to ping along with the music makers. Sara toyed with Dieskau's long, velvety ears, and sang to him.

Stan caught Lily laughing as she ducked under the arm of a tall, dancing, Indian guest. She signaled a 'look at me' expression to Stan. He acknowledged and shuffled across the floor in time with the music and asked Gisella, the neglected piano player's wife to dance. She said yes.

I was breathless from the vigorous dance and landed against Wolf as the first set of music ended. Hari announced in one language, then the other, they would now have a waltz for the "old folks to catch their breath." He counted one-two-three, one-two-three, and the musicians swayed to a gentle waltz. Husbands found their wives, Gisella and Liesel grabbed up Sara's hand, all bowed to each other and joined the dance.

Wolf closed his eyes and kissed my forehead. He lifted my left arm to his lips and kissed my healed new scar, from Alaska. "Thank you for staying with us while you healed up, my wife." I looked up and whispered in his ear. His sleepy eyes peeked open to say, "Ja, Liebchen?"

I whispered, "Who is Frau Graulich?"

Wolfgang asked, "Who?"

I said, "Frau Graulich, when you first kissed me in the Jeep. We were on our way to the Rose River, you mumbled something about Frau Graulich." I pulled back from his ear to look squarely into his face.

He asked again in a louder voice, "Who?"

The music was exuberant and loud. I rationalized that since I was Wolfgang's new bride, Frau Graulich was not someone to be worried about. We danced on.

*

Two days after the ceremony, the five Pennsylvanians were outbound. The local German and Indian guests had gone on to their own homes after the wedding party. Today's exodus convoy of vehicles headed to the airport showed Hans with Wolf and me and our luggage. Hari, with Liesel squeezed close to him, were in the number two car, carrying Lily and Stan and their bags. Gisella brought up the rear with Kimmy, Kevin, and sad to leave, Sara, all laughing, promising to return the favor next year in the U.S. The line of vehicles stacked to the roofs with luggage, swooshed through the gate in a cloud of dust and rumblings.

At the airport, the circle of friends and family became smaller as each waved good-bye, and headed for different departure gates. Cars and busses drove around the travelers pulling luggage from vehicles, and past the hugging couples.

I took Gisella's face between my palms and said, "Be sure to thank Hari again from me for being hostess to my daughter and her husband and Sara. Gisella, you have been so generous. I can't thank you enough." She pointed to the two girls hugging and jumping around in excitement. "It looks like they're finally happy with one another. Oh, Gisella, you were great, plus, you look spec-tac-ular. I'm so happy to have you for a new daughter-in-law."

Gisella whispered, "I'll deny I did this, but, I checked the flight times, the date, the plane's tail number, etc., etc. against every conceivable set of numbers, digit combinations, and the square root of B. You know how crazy we all are about numbers. Don't tell Dad. He'll be annoyed that burning my numbers didn't cure me. Maybe. Anyway, you're all clear." We laughed and hugged good-bye again.

Kimmy dragged the luggage on wheels and grabbed Sara's arm. Kevin scooped up the many pieces of loose baggage. All waved and headed for their plane. Stan and Lily had a later plane to catch, theirs going to Mumbai, for a little more vacation. Wolfgang stuffed a newspaper inside his suit jacket pocket and grabbed for my elbow, breaking up the daughter and wife hug and said in English, "Come along my wifey. I will do the next hugging. Good-bye, Gisella. You were a wonderful daughter for me. We thank you, over and over. See you in two weeks." He hollered in German over the traffic noise to Liesel, stationed in her father's Jeep. "Thank you, Little One, for helping us get married. We could not have done it without you. Take good care of your parents while we are gone." Liesel bounced up and down in her seat and waved.

Again he turned to Gisella, "Keep Hans and Hari busy. *Auf Wiedersehen, Liebschen.*"

Wolf escorted me through the crowd toward the plane departing at 2:00 p.m., or 1400, military time. No combination of numbers represented any significance. Smooth sailing ahead.

CHAPTER 26

FARE THEE WELL

All the seats in the waiting area were taken. Little children sped around, narrowly avoiding crashing into the luggage at the travelers' feet. Adults exchanged worried looks, knowing they'd soon be sharing a closed space with these same, noisy, energetic children. Wolf rested against a wall and closed his eyes. I leaned back against my husband, and with a satisfied enjoyment of the surroundings, faced the waiting room.

People stood in collections of language and nationality. The Germans were in robust conversations. An old white lady with a young Indian companion in a sari, smiled into the face of a chubby white man in a Yankee's baseball cap. She patted his hand. Students stood and leaned while balancing an open book or maneuvering a newspaper. Assorted business men were bent over their open briefcases, sorting and organizing, and an Elvis impersonator, clearly an entertainer, sat with two leggy, large-haired beautiful women. One of his ladies, in a grey business suit with a tiny skirt, cradled a small fluffy dog between the crook of her elbow and wrist. Her pretty nose nuzzled into the furry dog's head.

Two teen girls sat cross legged on the floor. They busied themselves, digging through their backpacks, then paging through their vacation photos. Their heads touched. Their

231

long hair falling forward, hid their faces. They laughed, rocked back, kicked their feet, and squealed at intervals. I enjoyed the girls and turned to Wolf. "Must be pictures of boys." I smiled and kissed him, punctuating my sentence.

The girls caught the kiss and together said in English, "Eeewww. Old people kissing. Gross." They rocked back and laughed another hearty laugh and turned their backs to the new Mr. and Mrs. Brucke, and continued paging through their photos.

The flight was boarding. Passengers lined up, flashed boarding passes and filed into the plane. The same two girls were in front of Wolf and me, and bumped their way down the narrow aisle of two seats per side, laughing and talking the whole way. I was happy to see we would not have to share our row of seats with a third person. Three's a crowd. Our seats were the very last in the tail section. He leaned to my ear, "I'm sorry for this back row, but these seats were all that was available when I booked the honeymoon."

I smiled. "I was thinking, how nice for a couple of honeymooners, back here in the shadows." My eyebrows signaled to Wolf that we were not alone. I whispered, "Except for those girls across the aisle."

I looked at the girls and spoke to them in English, "We must have been naughty to get the last seats in the back of the plane, huh?" The girls brightened at the English but had no verbal response. I thought, Good, Wolf and I can neck and outrage those two. We'll show them, 'Eeewww, old people kissing.'

I slid to my seat next to the window, pulled my seatbelt around my hips. As Wolf settled himself into his seat,

I ventured, "I hate to admit this, but my numbers thing is back. I haven't seen them recur, but I'm constantly thinking of them wondering when they'll reinsert themselves in my life. It's ridiculous. I thought the séance fixed it, but I still sometimes check and think about my numbers." He shot a bottom lip, poked-out, frown on my repentant expression. I continued, "I can't get over how the numbers led me, forced me to make certain decisions, and led straight to you. But, I have to stop obsessing about numbers. This is insanity. I mean it."

Wolfgang nodded. No other answer. He shoveled his backside left then right, digging in for a comfortable ride. Satisfied, he smiled again, and lengthened his seatbelt.

I took the seat voucher from Wolf and grabbed onto his hand, threading my fingers through his. I laughed and said, "Sure enough, like Gisella said, no number coincidences."

Wolf glanced at the voucher and said, "Mrs. Brucke, here comes the rest of our lives. Forget about numbers." He squeezed my hand and made a kiss in my direction.

"I'm buckled, Baby," I returned with a like kiss, "but who's counting?"

The liftoff was uneventful. After the juice and coffee service, I noticed my new husband's head was tipped back, his eyes almost closed and his mouth was gaping enough to insert an M&M. I had plenty more candies in my purse. He breathed long, even, relaxed breaths of someone who can sleep anywhere.

The rambunctious children who had been running around the waiting area were far forward in the plane and could not be heard. The girls across the aisle, no novices to travel, kicked off their shoes and punched up their sweaters to arrange makeshift pillows. One girl tipped to the window, her friend leaned to the other's shoulder.

An hour into the trip and five miles above the earth, I stirred from my leisurely paging through the airline's magazine when I glanced up between the seats in front of us. My attention was drawn to a flash of movement of bodies near the door to the cockpit. Voices were raised. I elbowed Wolf. "What's going on up front?"

Wolf had been undisturbed by the commotion and would have slept through except for my insistence that he get tuned in, and in a hurry. He poked his head to the aisle, then ducked behind the seat and with a rictus. He answered in a rapid whispered long stream of German. I ducked my head down and spat-whispered, "English. English." I emphasized my order with a punch to his upper arm.

Wolf frowned and rubbed his arm. Shrill voices from the front of the plane drifted back to us over the steady thrum of the plane's engines. A nasal, masculine voice at the front shouted words I could not understand, but his message silenced all the passengers' voices.

"What's up, Wolf?" I unclipped my seatbelt and stretched to peer over the top of the seat to see for myself the character standing with his back to the pilot's cabin. Wolf roughly yanked me back to my seat.

The threatening man stood with spread feet in a wide, rehearsed balance. He missed being unremarkable by being a little short and a bit too obese. His face missed being attractive by being too pink across his nose. His cheeks pushed up his tortoise shell glasses frames. A New York Yankees baseball cap, with its peak poking straight up, squashed his hair against his head except for the overgrown, greasy tufts over his ears that jutted straight out, giving him a clownish appearance. His khaki clothes were not overly rumpled or stained to indicate the wardrobe of a madman. His pockets revealed no bulges, although his torso was rounded by genetic bad luck, a lifetime of indiscretion or, worse, a vest of explosives. The significant article of clothing was his zipped flak jacket. He seemed to be alone. The passengers were quiet as the terrorist threatened those in the seats closest to him. He showed off a black, lethal looking weapon, fitting into the bend of his right arm to his hand. The man was all about his bad business.

"Can you understand what he's saying?" I shook my husband's sleeve. "What language?"

Wolf shook off my tugging. He whispered, "Bevff, for God's sake, be quiet. The man is insane. Be quiet. I think he's speaking English. Maybe, English. I can't tell."

I hung on to Wolf's arm with both hands. "Hey, I'll bet he's the guy I saw in the waiting area wearing a Yankee's baseball cap. I saw him bending to kiss an old white lady who was escorted by an Indian woman, maybe his rich old aunt and her companion."

"My, my, aren't you the mystery writer?" Wolf's lips didn't move as he whispered through the left side of his mouth.

I answered, "If the old lady were his mom, she would have given him a long, hard hug. She didn't. And the Indian woman stood back to give the employer privacy. Anyway, that's what I thought when I saw them together," I rattled off in a self-satisfied report.

"Shhh, Bevff. This is serious. Be quiet!"

The situation on the plane had come to an impasse. No one moved. The dog yapped a few times and was muffled. The terrorist squinted to the back of the plane, scanning his audience for possible problems.

The passengers were silent.

No bells summoned the flight attendants. No heads moved about, no one stood in the aisle to wait for the restroom. The little children were silent.

"Wolf, hear me out. He's alone, right?"

Wolf blinked agreement.

"Well, there's one of him and two of us, right? And more than that, there's a whole plane load of us. And Elvis. He's a big man."

Wolf shot a frowning glance at me.

"And Honey, this date, this plane, this time does not contain any of our numbers, right?"

Wolf's eyes squeezed shut.

I read, *Ahhh, good. A determined look.* "So, here's what we'll do."

"We'll do nossing, little lady," Wolf whispered in his thickest, most commanding German accent.

The terrorist signaled with his weapon for the two attendants huddled in the tail to come forward. The two young, Asian flight attendants spoke to each other, half crying as they walked in mincing steps toward the captor. Keeping his eyes on the two slender, elegantly tailored women, the lunatic growled, "You. Sit there." He pointed his rifle to the seat he'd vacated. He swung the barrel of his rifle toward one of the flight attendants. I could see him move quickly and I heard the young woman cry out, then whimper. She toppled backwards, out of my view. The other attendant screamed. He threw something at the second attendant and yelled, "Put them on each other. Go ahead, Do it!" The attendants who had greeted the fliers while boarding, were out of view. I don't know where they were.

"Wolf, come on. He's a pitiful amateur with a gun. The thing might not be loaded. Could even be a toy. Look at him. He's a misfit. He looks like a child molester; soft, short, fat, with glasses. Typical. Come on Wolf. Open your eyes."

"Not having a wife and kids at home does not make him more of head case. Shhhh...," he broke off.

"Quiet, back there. Quiet. I want you all to hear this before I send you all to Kingdom Come." He lifted his automatic weapon in a victory move to demonstrate his fire power to the passengers in the back. He diverted his attention from the full audience to pull an overloaded backpack from the floor next to his feet. The bag's heaviness was proven in his effort to hoist the satchel above his head for all to see. A tangle of rods and cords, looking like television renditions of TNT, spilled from the open flap of the canvas. "I am diverting this plane to Vietnam where we will show them who really won the war."

Do explosives look like that? The passengers whimpered and murmured. I looked across the aisle at the girls. Both had their heads tipped backwards with their mouths open in deep sleep. The blue airline blanket once pulled over one girl's shoulder had slipped to a heap at her feet.

The movie magazine lay open on the floor. Good, they're sleeping.

I tucked my head toward Wolf's shoulder, keeping below the crazy man's line of vision. I whispered, "Wolf, I'll go forward. He'll see a hysterical woman, crying, and calling. It'll throw him off. Maybe he'll threaten to kill me, but don't worry, it'll be a threat. You can see he's a wimp. He's not expecting some fifty-five-year-old tourist to screw up his terrorist plan. Anyway, when I get a few steps up the aisle, you hop out and act all worried about me, calling me back. I'll get to him before you catch up, and how about I start flashing my camera in his eyes, like in the movie, 'Rear Window?' You saw that movie? Right? Anyway, I'll flash his eyes and you'll overpower him. You'll be a hero. My hero. When he's down, the other passengers will hop in. I'll call them to help."

"Nein, No. No, Bevff, No. You must be crazy. This is crazy. He could kill you."

"Wolf. On this trip I had my luggage explode, I knocked my head on a heavy glass door, was pounded in the legs by a shot dog, had a bullet sear my arm, was spattered with fragments of glass, was accosted by branches on the dog-sled ride, vomited in front of a room full of singers, had my purse stolen, was in a dreadful bus and river accident, had the stuffing kicked out of me by a little kid, whose life I was saving. I got a button snagged in the balloon basket so I crouched down for most of the ride, ... and ... ," I stopped for breath, " ... and you're worried about some sawed off misfit with explosives? Come on, Give me a break. We can do this. And there's no numbers in this."

Made in the USA
Middletown, DE
12 September 2021